Turner has only one thing on his mind — killing the man who chained him and made his life hell. The problem is that Turner can't exactly announce what he's up to, and he can't ask for help, even though he sorely needs it. He can only continue training and hope it won't take him years to get his hands on Alpha Rhodes.

Raven was there when Turner was rescued, and he cares about the man. When his alpha's son asks him to check in on Turner, he can't say no. When his alpha asks him to train Turner and keep an eye on him because he knows what Turner is up to, his answer is still yes.

Neither of them expected to fall in love.

Turner can't afford to focus on Raven, and Raven can't allow Turner to kill anyone. Is their relationship doomed, or will they be able to find their way through the anger and need for revenge and realize they already have everything they need — each other?

This book is a work of fiction. Names, characters, places, and incidents either are products of the author's imagination or are used fictitiously. Any resemblance to actual events or locales or persons, living or dead, is entirely coincidental.

Everything He Needs
Copyright © 2021 Catherine Lievens
ISBN: 978-1-4874-3408-3
Cover art by Angela Waters

Published by eXtasy Books Inc

Look for us online at:
www.eXtasybooks.com

Everything He Needs
Allegheny Shifters 9

By

Catherine Lievens

CHAPTER ONE

Turner was going to die. His lungs were on fire and he couldn't breathe, yet, he continued running. He put one foot in front of the other, avoided a root poking from the ground, and tried to suck in a breath. His legs trembled and felt like they were about to break down on him, but nothing could stop him.

He *would* get his revenge.

He didn't care how long it took him or how much he had to train and put his body through this torture. Alpha Rhodes thought he was weak, but Turner wasn't. He'd never been, not even when Alpha Rhodes had forced his parents to hand him over so he could sell him. Turner needed to be stronger, though. If he was going to kill his old alpha, he needed all the strength and training he could get.

Unfortunately, he was doing it all on his own. He doubted the badger alpha would take it kindly if Turner explained what he wanted. Thomas was a good man, and he wouldn't want Turner to do this, not because of Alpha Rhodes, but because of Turner himself. He wouldn't want Turner to have to change himself to kill his old alpha, and Turner understood why.

That wasn't going to stop him.

He'd been thinking about killing Alpha Rhodes for so long that some days, it felt like he already had. Alpha Rhodes would never expect him to be able to get his hands on him, and Turner was going to take advantage of that. First, though, he'd become stronger.

He would never let himself be vulnerable again the way he had before. He would never allow anyone to trap him again, no matter who they were. He'd rather die.

He continued running through the forest, puffing and sweating. He'd been doing that since the carriers were allowed to leave the Bishop house, and with nothing better to do, it was perfect.

He knew that if he asked, Thomas would find him a job. He was tempted to look for one just because that way he wouldn't have to spend all his time at the Bishop house. But finding a job would mean focusing on something else, and he wasn't ready to do that. So instead, he spent most of his days running around the forest, then using the gym the badger enforcers used to keep themselves in shape. He'd gotten his fair share of strange glances, but he didn't care. He didn't owe anyone an explanation of what he was doing.

Turner should have been relieved that his current alpha was a good person, and he was. He knew Thomas would never hurt anyone, but he still couldn't ignore the fear something would happen to him and the other carriers if he wasn't careful. It didn't matter what kind of person Thomas was. After what Turner had been through, he knew what alphas were capable of.

And he hadn't even had the worst of it. Many of the carriers he'd been living with at the Bishop house had it worse than him, yet, they were dealing with it better than he was. That made him feel guilty, and at the same time, he wanted to protect them. None of them should have gone through what they did, not even him.

But he'd only been taken from his family and imprisoned in a shed. He hadn't been fed, and he'd known he would be sold as soon as his old alpha found a buyer. But what was it next to what Philip had gone through? Or Julian?

Turner was so focused on his thoughts that he didn't see

the second root. He should have been more careful. He'd been running in the forest long enough to know how harsh the ground was.

His foot caught, and he tilted forward so quickly he didn't even have the time to put his hands in front of him. His face hit the ground, pine needles and earth digging into his skin.

"Fuck," he muttered.

He stayed where he was, trying to get his breath back. If he'd been trying to hide what he was doing from everyone, he would have failed. Thankfully, the badgers were used to seeing him around the forest and at the gym, so they probably wouldn't even notice he was hurt.

Well, most of them wouldn't. Some definitely would, and Turner would have to deal with them. They'd have questions, and even though he could try not to answer, they'd push and push until he did. He supposed that was what being part of a group of people who cared about him meant. He wasn't used to it, and he wasn't sure he ever would. But in the meantime, it was kind of a bother.

He got back to his feet, wincing at the pain in his cheek. When he touched it, he felt dampness, which he was pretty sure was his blood. That was confirmed by his bloody fingers when he peered at them.

Great. Now there really would be no way for him to avoid talking about what had happened.

He rubbed his forearm against his cheek, streaking it with blood and dirt. He wasn't done running yet, but he didn't feel up to it anymore. He should continue, because if he gave up, he'd never get what he wanted. But he was so fucking tired. He'd been exhausted since he'd started training, and considering how much he'd done already, he doubted that taking one afternoon off would do damage.

Or at least, he hoped it wouldn't.

Instead of running back to the gym, he started walking. His

body hurt, and he felt like an old man of ninety instead of just twenty-seven. He wasn't sure if it was because of the training he'd been putting his body through or because of his past, and frankly, he didn't care. Why he felt that way didn't matter. The only thing that did matter was his goal, and with every day he trained, he was a little closer to getting what he wanted.

He hadn't realized how deep in the forest he'd gotten, but now that he had to walk, he did. Still, there was nothing to be done about it.

Instead of going back to the gym, he went to the Bishop house, since it was closer. He wasn't looking forward to explaining why he was in this state to any of his friends. They might not know why he was training, but they knew how important it was to him, and they'd understand. If they didn't, that was their problem, not Turner's.

He grimaced when he saw who was at the house. Of course Joel had to be there, checking in on the carriers who still lived there. He always did, and usually, Turner would have been happy to see him. But Joel had been making noises about Turner not being okay, and Turner knew him well enough to be sure he'd have questions. He was the alpha's son, and Turner couldn't exactly brush him off, no matter how much he might want to.

Joel and Misha were sitting on a bench on the porch. Both of them looked up when they heard Turner, but only Joel got to his feet. Misha tried to, but Turner glared at him until he sat his ass back on the bench. His stomach was so big that he looked like he was about to explode rather than give birth. Since he wasn't sure when he'd conceived, the healer couldn't know if he'd gone past his due date, but Turner would have been surprised if he hadn't. He was just too big to continue being pregnant for much longer.

"What happened to you?" Joel asked, rushing to Turner's

side and fussing over him.

Turner grunted. "Had an encounter with the ground."

Joel reached for Turner's cheek, but Turner took a step back. He didn't need to be taken care of. He could do it on his own.

Joel frowned. "You fell?"

"It's nothing. I'm fine."

"I'm sure you are. It doesn't mean you shouldn't let someone take care of you."

"I don't need you to. You're busy, and I just have to wash my face."

Joel leaned closer and looked at Turner's cheek. "I'm pretty sure there's stuff embedded in the wound. You'll need more than washing your face."

"And I'll do it on my own." Because that was how Turner was. He didn't have anyone in the world, not his parents, not his fellow skunks. The badgers had welcomed him, but was he really one of them?

He couldn't let himself to get used to this. He had to rely on himself and only himself.

Because when he didn't, people thought they could do whatever they wanted with him, and he would never allow that to happen again.

Raven laughed as he ducked the punch. Jacob glared at him and tried to kick him, but Raven danced away from his friend's foot. Then, since Jacob was distracted, Raven struck.

He hooked a leg behind Jacob's and pulled. Jacob yelped and fell to the ground, and before he could get back on his feet, Raven sat on his chest, straddling it. He wiggled his eyebrows, then made a show of looking around. "I hope Chris isn't here."

Jacob grunted and tried to push Raven away, but Raven

wasn't going anywhere.

"Even if he were, he'd know I don't want you on top of me. That's his place alone," Jacob muttered.

Raven grimaced. "That's disgusting. I don't want to listen to you talk about your sex life."

Jacob grinned and suddenly rolled them until Raven was under him, his back flat on the mats. "That's because you're jealous. When was the last time you were with someone?"

Raven quickly raised his knee, aiming for Jacob's groin. Jacob managed to push away before Raven's knee could touch him. He rolled onto his back, then got to his feet and faced Raven again.

Raven rubbed his forearm on his face, trying to get the sweat out of his eyes. Both he and Jacob were panting, but Raven was having fun. He knew he was probably one of the few who was, but his job was his life. He protected the cete. And to do that, he needed to train. He hadn't turned soft like Jacob had since he'd met and fallen in love with Chris. Raven didn't have anyone in his life, and he was glad.

Someone clapped their hands, and both Raven and Jacob stopped moving. Alex stood by the mats, nodding. "Good."

"Why are we even doing this?" someone complained from the other side of the gym.

Raven glared at them, even though he wasn't sure who had spoken.

Alex's expression hardened. "Doing what?"

Whoever had spoken was smart enough to realize they shouldn't answer. The silence stretched out, making everyone uncomfortable. Raven wasn't. Alex knew how dedicated he was to their cause and their team.

"You want to know why we're still training?" Alex asked. "Apart from the fact that our job is to defend our people, have you forgotten why you're part of this team?"

Alex looked around. No one answered.

"My father created this team to help save the carriers. Now, I realize that with almost all the alphas who hurt the carriers gone and the council finally working for us rather than against us, you might believe we're not needed anymore. Hopefully, you're right. But let's not forget that at least one of the old alphas is still in place, and the council wasn't able to charge him with what he did in the past. He's free and still leading his people, and it would be easy for him to hurt more people, especially carriers. And even if we don't consider him, what about everyone else in the forest? Do you truly believe that one law will be enough for the carriers to have a perfect life? Don't you think that no matter what the council orders, some people will never accept that carriers belong in the forest or treat them like everyone else? Frankly, it surprises me that so far, all the carriers we know have been allowed to go home."

Some had gone, but others hadn't. The Bishop house wasn't as crowded as it had been in the beginning when Thomas had decided it would be a haven for carriers. A few of the carriers had gone back to their people, while others had accepted Thomas's offer to move into their own home in badger territory. Most of those had found love, and they were building families.

But a few remained — mostly those who had been sold and hurt by their own alphas. Raven could understand not wanting to go back and being afraid that a new leader would hurt them no matter how different from the old one he was. They were safe at the Bishop house, and Thomas would never kick them out. They had a home with the badgers, no matter what happened.

"We're protectors," Alex continued. "That's why we became part of this team."

Jacob shuffled his feet. He wasn't part of the team, but he was still a guard for the cete. They didn't protect the same people, but that didn't make him less of a protector than everyone else here.

"But if you'd rather not do this anymore, you're welcome to talk to my father or me. We'll find someone to replace you."

"That won't be necessary," Valerie said.

She looked around, as if daring whoever had spoken before to contradict her. No one did.

With a nod from Alex, the tension broke. The team members started talking again, and a couple glared at Alastair, the bat member of their team. Raven wasn't surprised he'd been the one to complain. Bats always complained.

Since this team had been created to help all the carriers, it was made up of different shifters. Besides Alex, Raven was the only badger. He didn't mind. He'd become friends with almost the entire team and friendly with the others. Besides, they weren't here to be friends. They were here to protect the carriers, and they had. Now that the forest seemed to be at peace, they didn't have a lot of work to do anymore, but Raven didn't care. Like Alex said, until the carriers were treated like every other shifter in the forest, the team would have a reason to exist, and he'd be on it.

His thoughts flashed back to when Kari had brought the team to free Turner, but he quickly pushed those away. He couldn't focus on just one carrier, not when so many of them needed help.

Since the team was disbanding, Raven made his way to Alex. He was talking to Valerie, but she nodded at Raven and stepped away when she saw him.

Alex smiled. "Raven. Good job on the mats."

Raven grinned. "You know I always enjoy beating Jacob's ass."

Alex laughed. "Just be careful of Chris."

"I can take him, too." Raven hesitated. He wanted to talk, but he wasn't sure there was anything they could do. "About

Alpha Rhodes," he began.

Alex's smile disappeared, and he sighed heavily. "I know. I want to lock his ass up as much as you do, but as far as I know, he hasn't done anything against the law since the council created them."

"We should have killed him when we had the opportunity," Raven muttered.

"I suppose we might have another chance, but he's been following the rules, so for now, there's nothing we can do."

"You know he's planning something. And if he's not, he's laughing behind our backs because he's allowed to do whatever he wants with no consequences. You saw what he did to Turner. You were there when we found him."

Alex clasped Raven's shoulder. "How is he?"

"I don't know." Because Raven was avoiding Turner. He still wasn't sure why Turner had felt comfortable enough to let him free him from the shed, but he'd wanted to give Turner space, and now, it was easier just to stay away.

"Look, at the moment, Rhodes is on his own. He's isolated, because all the other alphas are working with my father and the council. I doubt there's a lot he can do on his own."

Raven wasn't convinced of that. "But we're still keeping an eye on him, right?"

Alex squeezed and let go. "Always. You know my father. He won't rest until he's sure that everyone who hurt a carrier is gone from the forest, one way or another."

Raven was grateful he had one of the best alphas in the forest, but it still didn't feel like enough. Thomas's hands were tied, as were the council's. They couldn't do anything to Rhodes, not unless they wanted to go against their own rules.

Maybe it was time to do just that.

"Turner?"

Turner managed to suppress his groan, but it was a close thing. He plastered a smile on his face and turned to face Joel, who was standing just inside Turner's bedroom. "I thought I'd closed the door," Turner said.

Joel looked sheepish. "You did."

"Yet here you are, inside my bedroom."

"I wouldn't be here if I weren't worried about you. Turner, please. You have to see this isn't healthy."

Turner crossed his arms over his chest. "I'm not sure what you're talking about."

"You know what I'm talking about, and you're ignoring it." Joel sucked in a breath. "I know I can never understand what you and the others went through. I might be a carrier, but I was lucky enough that my father loved me and did everything he could to protect me and give me the best life he could. I can only imagine what your life was even before Alpha Rhodes stuck you in that shed. But you're free now."

"I'm aware of that." The fact that he wasn't stuck in that shed anymore was a big indicator of it.

Joel shook his head. "I'm not sure you are, because even though you're free, you're acting as if you're still in that shed."

"I have no idea what you're talking about."

Joel closed and leaned against the door as if afraid Turner would try to escape. "Your body is free, but your mind isn't."

This time, Turner did groan. "Can we not talk about this?"

"I don't think it's right not to talk about it, especially when it's obvious something is wrong with you. Look at everyone else. Now that they're free, they're starting to build their life."

"I'm happy for them."

"We all are. You're not doing anything like that, though."

"How can you say that?"

"From watching you. The only thing you're doing is training, and while I think I understand where it comes from, it's not healthy. You're not planning your future or making decisions about what your next step will be. Instead, your entire energy is into training. I realize you don't want to feel weak, but everyone knows you're not, and you're going to hurt yourself if you continue this way." His gaze lingered on Turner's face. "You already have."

"It was just a scratch," Turner protested.

"This time, sure. What about next time?"

"I was running, not fighting."

Although that wasn't a bad idea. Turner wouldn't have been able to hold his own against anyone when he first arrived here, but now? He just might. He had no idea how to fight, but that didn't mean he couldn't at least try. He'd need to find someone to teach him how and train him, but with so many badgers around, he didn't think he'd have a problem.

Not with most of them, anyway. As long as Joel stayed out of Turner's business, everything would be fine. Turner didn't want to tell Joel that, though. No matter how annoyed he was at what Joel was doing, he understood where it came from. Joel cared about Turner and about everyone else in the Bishop house — hell, in cete territory, and maybe in the entire forest — and he acted accordingly, which meant he tried taking care of people. But Turner could take care of himself, and he needed Joel and everyone else to realize that and stop trying to tell him what to do.

Unfortunately, that was easier said than done.

Turner sucked in a breath, trying to find the best words not to offend Joel or hurt him while getting what he wanted.

"I appreciate you caring about me," he eventually said.

Joel snorted. "Don't try telling me that you don't hate me because I'm sticking my nose in your business."

To his own surprise, Turner laughed. It had been a while since he'd laughed, and he hadn't realized he could still make that sound. "I can't say I enjoy it, and I'm sure you understand why."

"I do. I wouldn't be doing this if I wasn't worried about you."

"And I know you're worried because you're my friend. That, I appreciate. But like you said, I'm supposed to start making plans for my life and my future, and I can't have you holding my hand through the entire thing. I have to learn to stand up on my own."

"But don't you see? You don't have to stand up on your own." Joel hesitated. "I might not understand everything you and the others have been through, but I do know how it feels to be vulnerable. Even though I knew my father loved my brother and me and that he'd do everything he could to protect us, there was still the fear that someone would find out about us and we'd be in trouble. Back then, the council wouldn't have hesitated to take us away from our home, and both Levi and I were terrified. It was just luck that we weren't forced away and that we didn't end up in the kind of situation you and the others ended up in. It's not the same, and it never will be. But I want you to remember that even if you accept help from someone, it doesn't make you weak. It makes you human, and it means there are people who care about you. Isn't that worth having?"

Of course it was, but Turner didn't say it.

He'd never had this. His parents loved him, but they hadn't been able to protect him against their alpha. When Alpha Rhodes had found out Turner was a carrier, he'd ordered Turner's parents to hand him over, and they had. Not doing it would have meant trouble for them, and they couldn't afford it.

So they'd given Turner away.

Turner had been kept in that shed for weeks, maybe longer. He'd never done the math, and he had no intention of ever doing it. What he did know for sure was that he'd been starved and been about to be sold like cattle. He hated Alpha Rhodes for that, but also for taking his family from him. Even now that he was free, Turner couldn't contact them, not when Alpha Rhodes was still in charge of the surfeit. If Turner even tried to visit, he'd pay for it. He didn't know if Alpha Rhodes would capture or hurt him—especially not when the council and the cete protected Turner, but he wasn't willing to take the risk.

Not yet. Not until he was sure he could kill Alpha Rhodes.

Joel sighed. "Just remember I'm here for you and that I'm not the only one. Everyone in the house and the cete wants you to be happy. You have all the time you need to find out what that means and how to achieve it. Don't obsess over the past. Try to focus on the future and on what you can have."

Turner nodded but didn't look at Joel again. He waited and listened to Joel leave. When the door closed behind him, Turner allowed himself to relax.

He was touched that Joel cared so much about him, and he desperately wanted to focus on his future. He couldn't do that when Alpha Rhodes was still around, living his life and hurting people. As long as he was there, Turner would always be terrified he'd find him and hurt him again. That was why he couldn't focus on his future. To be able to do that, he'd have to be sure Alpha Rhodes couldn't hurt him or anyone else, and the only way it would happen was if Alpha Rhodes died.

Since no one seemed to be about to get rid of him, Turner would do it himself. He wasn't ready yet, far from it, but he wasn't afraid of hard work or pain. He'd have to go through a lot of both before he was ready, but it wouldn't be enough to stop him.

"Where's your boyfriend?" Alastair teased.

Raven frowned. "Who are you talking about? Jacob isn't

my boyfriend." Just the thought made Raven feel sick.

He and Jacob had been best friends since they were kids, and as far as Raven was concerned, he'd never thought about anything more. It might sound stupid, but Jacob might as well have been his brother.

"Not him. That guy we rescued from the shed."

Raven narrowed his eyes. "You mean Turner?"

Alastair didn't look like he wanted to answer, but he nodded. "Yeah, him. He seemed to like you when we found him."

For a moment, Raven resisted the urge to slam Alastair against the wall. Alex was still there, giving a few pointers to Terrence and Flynn, who'd fought after Raven and Jacob. He wouldn't take it kindly if Raven beat Alastair's face into the floor, but Raven couldn't let this go. Besides, he was known as a hothead. Alex wouldn't be surprised.

Raven grabbed the collar of Alastair's t-shirt, turned around, and slammed him against the wall. He heard the breath whoosh out of Alastair's lungs, but that didn't stop him from putting all his weight against him. This way, Alastair couldn't take a full breath.

Then Raven glared. "You were talking about Turner, a guy who was taken from his family and locked in a shed before he could be sold to another alpha, who would then have raped him until he got pregnant."

"I didn't mean—"

"The problem with you, Alastair, is that you often say things you don't mean, or rather, that you don't think before speaking. You believe that because most of the alphas have been dealt with, the carriers aren't in danger anymore? You think that Alpha Rhodes isn't a danger to Turner?"

"I never said that," Alastair choked out.

"You didn't have to say it in those words for everyone here to know that's what you think. But fine. Let's ignore that and focus on what you *are* saying about Turner."

14

"I didn't mean anything bad. I just know he likes you."

"Because he clung to me when we found him? Is it because he likes me, or because to him, I represented safety and freedom? He and the other carriers went through a lot, and they don't deserve to be talked about the way you just did. Got it?"

Alastair nodded eagerly. His face was turning red, and Raven knew he had to let go.

He didn't want to.

It pissed him off, and it wasn't just Alastair. He'd heard other people talk about carriers as if now that there was a law against hurting them, they were just like everyone else. That wasn't the case, because people didn't treat them like everyone else. It wasn't fair to them, not after everything they'd gone through, and Raven would be damned if he let anyone talk badly about any of them, but especially Turner.

Raven didn't understand why, but Turner had a special place in his heart and mind. Maybe it was because he was the only one who'd so obviously latched onto him and had trusted him to keep him safe, or maybe it was because of something else. Raven didn't think it mattered. The only thing that mattered was that he cared about Turner and wanted to keep him safe.

"That's enough," Alex said.

Raven took a step back and dumped Alastair to the floor. Alastair sucked in a breath and looked at Alex, his eyes wide. "We were just joking around," he said.

Raven begrudgingly nodded at him in thanks. It would have been easy for Alastair to demand that Raven pay for this, and Alex wouldn't have been able to say no.

"Thank you, Alastair. I think you and the rest of the team should head to the showers."

Raven started to turn around to obey, but Alex caught his arm. "Not you," he murmured.

So Raven waited. He hoped Alex wasn't about to kick him

off the team, but that was a possibility. Raven should have thought before doing that, but he'd been pissed, and he still was.

He wanted to do more. What good was it for him to be on this team when they couldn't get rid of Rhodes?

"What's going on?" Alex asked once they were alone.

"We already talked about this. I'm frustrated, all right? It's not right that Alpha Rhodes is still around, free to do whatever he wants, when he and his friends terrified so many carriers. They're still afraid to leave the Bishop house because of what was done to them and what could happen to them in the future. And what are we doing? We're training and fucking around, unable to do anything else."

"I understand how frustrated you are, and trust me, we all are. But I won't work with a loose cannon, Raven. If you can't play nice and work with the other team members, I'll have to take you off the team."

Maybe that was what Raven needed. Maybe he could go after Rhodes and anyone else who deserved it on his own.

But no. Doing that would make him a pariah, and that wasn't what he wanted. At the end of the day, the cete and the forest were his home. He didn't want to lose that, not even to kill Rhodes. The man didn't deserve Raven to put all of that on the line for him.

"I just think he needs to pay," he said.

"I agree. He should be in jail and unable to hurt anyone else. We still don't know what's going on in skunk territory, and he won't permit us to check in on his skunks. We're doing everything we can within the law, and you know that. If we try doing anything else, he could turn it against us. And what would happen then? The team would be disbanded, and it'd be even easier for him to do whatever he's planning."

"What are we supposed to do, then?"

"Continue working. It's the *only* thing we can do, no matter how much you don't feel like it. Eventually, he's going to do the wrong thing, and we'll be there to catch him."

"And in the meantime, he can do whatever he wants."

"In his territory, yes. I don't like it any more than you, but it's not something we can do anything about at the moment. I don't want to lose you as a team member, but you have to stop doing this. I know Alastair can be a dickhead, but he's not a bad guy."

"I wouldn't be too sure about that," Raven muttered.

"He's not," Alex insisted. "You haven't given him or anyone else on the team a chance, though. I know you're not in this to make friends, but would it be so bad if you did? You have to trust the people you work with, and they have to trust you. How will you make that happen when you slammed him against the wall and threatened him?"

"He shouldn't be talking about Turner."

"I agree, but I also think you're sensitive when it comes to Turner." Alex hesitated. "It's none of my business, but have you talked to him recently?"

"No. I don't want to scare him."

"I see. I've been talking to Joel, and he's worried about Turner. He's not doing well."

Raven frowned. "Is he ill?"

"Not physically. He's having a hard time dealing with everything, though. He's taking it out on his body by overtraining, and Joel's afraid something will break eventually."

"I'm not sure why you're telling me this."

Alex smiled. "I don't know. I just thought you should know."

Raven didn't understand Alex most of the time, but he didn't have to. Alex was his superior, so he obeyed orders, even when they weren't obvious. If Alex had told him about Turner, it was because he wanted Raven to visit him.

So Raven would. It wouldn't be a hardship, since he

wanted to see Turner anyway.

CHAPTER TWO

Turner was used to visitors. Now that the carriers weren't in danger anymore, the Bishop house was open to anyone who wanted to come. Mostly it was badgers since the house was in their territory, but the carriers had made friends with other people, usually through other carriers.

Turner never had visitors. He didn't want anyone from his old life to visit him, and he thought he'd run away screaming if they tried. He wasn't used to anyone seeking him out, and he was grateful for that, because he wouldn't have known how to behave.

That was why he didn't know what to say when he walked into the living room and found Raven sitting on the couch.

It was obvious Raven was as uncomfortable as Turner. He was sitting on the edge of the couch, his fingers linked together in his lap. It looked like he was ready to run at any second, and Turner suspected that was the case.

Around him, carriers were settled on the couches and armchairs. Misha was right next to Raven, which would explain some of the awkwardness. Raven didn't look like he knew what to do with the pregnant man, and Turner suspected it would be no use to tell him he didn't have to do anything special.

Gallagher, Oakley, and Hector were also in the room, and all of them were staring at Raven.

Turner cleared his throat, and everyone jumped and looked at him. Raven shot to his feet, looking both relieved and uncomfortable.

"What's going on here?" Turner asked.

"Raven is here to see you," Gallagher answered.

Turner frowned. "Why?"

"He wouldn't tell us."

"I just wanted to check on you," Raven said. He rubbed the back of his neck and avoided looking at Turner.

"Why don't we go outside?" Turner suggested, taking pity on the man.

Raven nodded eagerly. "That would be great." He almost ran out of the room, but Turner didn't follow him right away. Instead, he turned to look at the other carriers.

"What did you tell him that terrified him so much?"

Misha laughed. "I don't think it's anything we said, but rather, my presence next to him. He kept looking at my stomach as if he expected the baby to pop out at any second and to have to be the one to catch it."

"He might have had to," Turner pointed out.

Misha rubbed his stomach. "I can't wait for this to be over."

Talking about pregnancy made Turner uncomfortable, especially in Misha's case, because everyone knew how Misha had gotten pregnant. An alpha had bought and raped him, and he'd still be there if Kari hadn't intervened. Misha didn't seem to care, though. He loved his baby, and he was eager to become a father. Turner might not understand it, but he didn't have to.

"Is he your boyfriend?" Oakley asked.

"Raven? He's just a friend."

Although Turner wasn't sure he could even call him that. Raven *wasn't* a friend. He'd been there when Turner had been rescued, and he'd been the one Turner had latched onto. Turner still didn't understand why, and he wasn't about to analyze his feelings. He just knew that he felt safe with Raven, whether or not he should.

They'd seen each other from a distance since then, but they

hadn't spoken, which made Raven's presence here even more puzzling. It might be Turner's only possibility to do something about his training, though, so he left the living room and headed outside.

Raven was on the porch, leaning against the railing. One of his legs was up, his foot against the wood, and his jeans tight around his thigh.

He looked good. Turner couldn't deny Raven was attractive, even though he was doing his best not to think about that kind of thing. He couldn't afford a boyfriend, and he didn't want one, not even one as attractive as Raven.

Raven had to be in his mid-thirties, maybe a bit younger. Both his eyes and his hair were dark, although a few silver strands in his hair hinted at his age. He was taller than Turner and much more muscled.

But instead of being afraid of that, Turner felt safe with him, and he wanted Raven to wrap his arms around him and hold him close like he had when he'd rescued him.

Turner shook his head. "We're alone. What did you want to tell me?"

Raven looked away. "I just wanted to check how you are."

It took Turner a moment to understand why. "Joel talked to you?"

"No, he didn't."

"Someone did, though."

"Alex mentioned Joel being worried about you."

Turner crossed his arms over his chest. "And you decided you should check on me? Why?"

"Not check on you. I just thought I'd see how you were."

"Isn't that the definition of checking in on me?"

He wasn't sure why he was giving Raven a hard time. He wasn't the only one who wanted to make sure Turner was okay, and he wouldn't be the last one, either.

But Turner needed to focus on getting strong and training.

He needed to focus on Alpha Rhodes and killing him, and that wouldn't happen if he got distracted by someone like Raven.

Turner opened his mouth to tell Raven that he was fine and didn't need to check in on him, but Raven beat him to it.

"Why don't we shift and have a run in the forest?" he asked.

"You want to shift with me?"

"Isn't that what I just said? We could have some fun, just the two of us. Unless you're uncomfortable with me? I could tell you not to be afraid of me, but I know it's not as easy as that."

Turner shook his head. "I'm not afraid of you." If anything, Raven was one of the few people Turner trusted.

He didn't understand it, but he suspected it had to do with Raven being there when he'd been rescued. He hadn't been the only one, but Turner had latched onto him. It could have been anyone else, he supposed.

It hadn't been.

"I'm sorry. I don't have the time to shift," he said.

Unfortunately, that wasn't enough for Raven to back off. "What do you mean? Do you have a job?"

"I could. You don't have to sound so surprised."

"That's not what I meant. It's just that I haven't heard about you or any of the other carriers here having one."

"Look," Turner said. He was starting to lose his patience. "No, I don't have a job, but it doesn't mean I don't have things to do. I do, and that means I don't have time to shift and go running in the forest."

Turner thought that would be enough to get Raven to leave, but he should have known better. Nothing was ever easy in his life, and he doubted that would ever change.

Instead of going away, Raven pushed off from the railing and came to stand in front of Turner. "What are you hiding?"

he asked.

"Nothing. But even if I was hiding something, it would be none of your business."

"You're right. It *is* none of my business. But I promised Alex I'd check in on you, and if I tell him and Thomas I'm worried about you, they'll start sticking their noses into whatever you're doing. Is that what you want?"

Dammit. It definitely wasn't.

Turner was hiding something, and Raven wanted to find out what it was. He was tempted to push, but he wouldn't. Turner was still dealing with what happened to him, and Raven didn't wish to worsen the situation. He wanted Turner to have the privacy he hadn't had with Rhodes and for him to be able to trust him. That wouldn't happen if he pushed too much, no matter how tempted he was.

Still, he thought it would be good for Turner to go out there and shift for a while. As far as he knew, Turner hadn't done that in a long time, if ever, since he arrived in cete territory. Turner might not believe he needed it, but every shifter needed to shift every so often. It would be good to leave everything behind for a while, but Raven would have to convince him of that first.

"We don't have to stay away for long," he promised, trying to coax Turner into saying yes. "I understand having things to do. I do have a job, you know?"

To Raven's delight, Turner's cheeks turned pink. "I'm aware of that. I never said you didn't have a job."

"So you're aware that I have things to do, too. Everyone here has something to do, but we find time to shift. Even Thomas does, and he's the alpha. You're not going to tell me you have less time than the alpha?"

Turner glared. "You won't leave me alone until I agree, will you?"

"I don't know. Are you willing to risk it?"

Turner huffed. "Fine. We'll go out there and shift for a while. As long as you promise you'll leave me alone once we're done."

"I swear I will."

He heard Turner grumble something about not believing him, but he didn't care. He'd won, at least for now.

He gestured at the porch steps. "After you."

He wasn't sure if Turner would be more comfortable having him in front of him or behind, but Turner didn't even hesitate. He stomped down the porch steps and headed toward the forest without looking back. Raven followed him, amused at Turner's temper.

He hadn't seen much of it when he and the others had rescued Turner, but then there hadn't been an opportunity. Turner had been terrified and in bad shape—underfed, cold, and scared. Now he was none of that, except maybe scared. He didn't look like it at the moment, but he might just be trying not to show it. Knowing what he did about Turner, Raven wouldn't be surprised if that was the case.

It wouldn't be helpful to tell Turner not to be afraid, so Raven kept his mouth shut and followed Turner's lead. Turner walked into the forest like he knew where he was going, and he probably did. Raven had briefly talked to Joel before coming, and he'd mentioned that Turner spent most of his time either at the gym or in the forest running around and training. He'd been worried, and Raven was, too, but it didn't mean that whatever Turner was doing was bad. Maybe training helped him feel more secure, and Raven was all for that if it was true. There was such a thing as overdoing it, though, and he was here to make sure that wasn't what Turner was doing.

After a moment, Turner stopped walking. Raven looked around, curious and not surprised to see that while they were still close to the house, they were far enough that no one would bother them.

"Is this fine?" Turner asked.

"It's perfect. We're close to the border. Have you ever tried to spy on the humans on the other side?"

Turner snorted. "I have enough problems on my own without adding whatever humans are doing."

"I can't say I disagree. Still, aren't you curious?"

Turner shrugged. "So what if I am?"

"Nothing."

Raven reached for the bottom of his shirt and pulled it off. Turner's eyes widened, looking away, but Raven had noticed it. He didn't know what it meant or if it meant anything at all, but since he wasn't here to seduce Turner, he focused on undressing instead.

Still, he couldn't help but sneak glances at Turner or notice that Turner was doing the same.

As soon as he was naked, Raven shifted into his badger form. He stretched and grinned, trying to remember the last time he'd done it. It had been too long, and since he'd just scolded Turner for not shifting often enough, he really should remember to do it more often himself.

When Turner stripped, too, Raven turned to face him. He took a moment to look at him, trying to understand how Turner was.

He hadn't been wearing much the last time Raven had been in close contact with him when they'd found him in that shed. He'd been too thin, having almost starved. He'd also been dirty and terrified, but he wasn't now. Instead, he looked good, and all the training he was doing was obvious.

He wasn't tall, but he was lithe, with long muscles and legs. There was a hint of a six-pack on his stomach, and Raven's gaze moved from that to the trail of hair, to Turner's cock.

Then Turner shifted.

Raven was relieved and berated himself for creeping on Turner. This wasn't what they were here for. He'd managed to convince Turner to come into the forest to shift, and that was what they were going to do. There would be no ogling, not again, or at least, that was what Raven promised himself.

He hoped he'd be able to keep that promise.

As soon as Turner was in his skunk form, Raven moved closer to him. He rubbed his head against Turner's, silently telling him he was there and that he cared about him. He couldn't explain why, and he wasn't going to try. He didn't care why Turner was so important to him or what it meant for both of them. He just wanted Turner to know he was there and that he always would be.

Turner made a strange sound and took a step back. For a moment, Raven thought he'd done the wrong thing and maybe moved too close to Turner and made him uncomfortable. It only lasted a moment, because then Turner moved toward Raven, hesitantly rubbing back.

Raven found himself grinning, which he knew could look a bit odd in his badger form. Turner didn't seem to care and smiled back before turning around and rushing between the trees.

Raven went after him.

Turner was a gorgeous skunk. His fur was black and white, the stripes evident in the forest. Even if they hadn't been, Raven would have been able to find him. It was what he was trained to do. He didn't have to try hard, though. He suspected Turner was making it easy to see him, which was kind of funny considering, who they were. Maybe Turner didn't want to waste time because he had things to do, or maybe he just wanted to have fun. Whatever the reason behind how he was acting, it didn't matter.

Raven ran behind the trees, acting as if he couldn't see Turner. Then, he twirled around and jumped onto him.

Turner squeaked and ran away. It was hard to judge what Turner felt, since they were in their animal forms, so Raven hoped he hadn't scared him. He followed Turner, and they continued playing in the forest for a while. It was nothing Raven hadn't done with other people, generally friends, but it still felt different. It was good to see Turner having fun, and that was what Raven focused on.

Eventually, they reached the fence that separated the forest from the human world. Since Turner hadn't seemed interested before, Raven expected him to turn around and head back. Instead, he stopped next to the fence. To Raven's surprise, he shifted. Raven quickly did the same, not wanting Turner to be uncomfortable because he was the only one naked. Turner was a shifter, so he should be used to being naked around other shifters, but with what had happened to him, Raven wasn't sure.

Then the situation was awkward in a different way because now Raven couldn't avoid looking at Turner's naked body. Turner didn't seem to notice. He was focused on what was outside of the forest as he linked his fingers into the fence. "You know, sometimes, I wonder if their life is really like what we see on TV," he said.

Raven shrugged. "Probably not. Those are movies and things like that. I mean, the stuff they think about how *we* live is all wrong."

Turner chuckled. "That's true. We don't live in caves."

Raven remembered that particular documentary. It shouldn't have been called that, but rather a movie, and it had made him and his friends laugh every time they thought about it. It had been either that or accepting that humans saw them as savages and nothing more, which had disturbed Raven more than he wanted to admit.

"Humans are stupid," he said with a grunt.

Turner didn't answer. Instead, he continued watching the

world outside of the fence.

Turner hadn't been lying when he'd said he didn't think about humans and their world often. His life was complicated enough as it was, and obsessing over humans would only make it more complicated. Still, sometimes he wondered. What did humans think about life in the forest? What would Turner and the other shifters think about how humans lived?

The first question would be fairly easy to answer. Turner just had to go find the humans who now lived in the forest with them and ask. He doubted any of them would be offended, and if he truly was afraid of offending them, he could ask Josiah's boyfriend. The man was as human as they came, yet, he didn't have a problem living with Josiah and having a family with him. They hadn't been together long, but they fit like they belonged together, and it gave Turner hope.

Josiah had been through a lot. Both his brother and his father had abused him, yet, he had everything Turner wanted.

He was the alpha of his band. He was in love with a man who loved him back, and, together, they were about to start a family. Turner wasn't sure that was what he wanted, but that wasn't what he was jealous of.

He wanted it, but only in the sense that he wanted to be free to make his own decisions. He technically was. He was living at the Bishop house, could decide what he wanted to do—if he wanted to find a job, to move out of the Bishop house and get his own home. He'd do that, eventually.

But he had to get rid of Alpha Rhodes first. He'd never be able to feel safe if he didn't, and that meant he couldn't start his new life until Alpha Rhodes was dealt with.

Turner didn't want to think about that right now. This wasn't an opportunity he often allowed himself. Usually, when he wasn't training, he was resting, plotting how to kill his old alpha, or cooking. He needed to sustain his body through the training, so it was better to cook for himself. Usually, he ended up cooking for everyone, which wasn't a bad thing. Misha especially needed nutrition, since he was pregnant.

So he didn't often allow himself to have this distraction, take time off and just walk in the forest and play around.

"Thank you," he murmured.

"What are you thanking me for?" Raven asked.

Turner liked how Raven's presence made him feel. He didn't know why Raven made him feel safe, but he did, and that was all Turner cared about. He knew nothing would happen to him as long as he was with Raven.

"For forcing me to do this."

Raven snorted. "I forced you, huh?"

"Well, you wouldn't take no for an answer, so you kind of did."

"I wouldn't have insisted if I hadn't believed it would be good for you. And it is, isn't it?"

"It is," Turner begrudgingly agreed. "I needed time away from everything, but I didn't realize it."

"You do now." Raven hesitated. "You can call me, you know. If you want to do this again, or if you need anything else. I know I probably remind you of a time you never want to think about again, but I'm here for you if you need anything."

Turner was touched. A lot of people had helped since he'd arrived in badger territory, and sometimes, he still wondered why. What had he done to deserve it? How could these people be so good to him and the other carriers? "Thank you. And no, you don't remind me of things I'd rather not think about."

"I find that hard to believe."

"I do, too, but it's the truth. I feel safe with you."

Raven looked surprised, and frankly, Turner shared that

feeling. He hadn't lied, though. He did feel safe with Raven, and since that didn't happen often, he wasn't going to give up whatever he and Raven had.

And Raven was a protector. He was part of the team that had been put together to rescue the carriers, so he knew what he was doing. Could he help Turner? Turner didn't want to ask, because he was afraid Raven would say no, but he wouldn't find out if he didn't, so he might as well try.

"You know I've been training," he started, trying to find the best way to ask.

"That's why Joel sent me."

Turner glared. "I'm going to have to talk to him about boundaries again."

Raven laughed. "I've known him since we were children. It's not going to work. When Joel worries about someone, he throws his entire self into helping that person. Unfortunately for you, you're one of those people."

Turner couldn't let himself be derailed by this new topic. "I understand why he's doing it, and I'm even grateful, but I need him to take a step back."

Raven frowned. "But you understand why he's worried, right?"

Turner nodded curtly. "I do." And he had to admit Joel was right to be worried, considering what he was planning. He already knew what Raven's answer would be if he told him he wanted to kill Alpha Rhodes, so he wouldn't even mention it. Instead, he said, "Do you want to know why I've been training?"

"I think both Joel and I can guess."

"I never want to feel as weak and vulnerable as I was when I was in that shed." And that was the truth. Turner's main goal was to kill his old alpha, but it wasn't the only one. He needed to feel strong and to be able to defend himself.

Raven nodded. "That's what I thought. But you realize you

were never weak, right?"

"We'll have to disagree on that. But since you understand where I'm coming from, I was wondering if you could help me."

"What do you need help with?"

"Training. I've been doing what I can, looking on the Internet, but I really have no idea what I'm doing. I need help taking this to the next level."

"And you want *me* to help you?"

Turner moved to face Raven. "Who better than you? You're part of the team that rescued me. You're one of the few people I fully trust, even though I don't understand why. I know it's not going to be easy and that you're busy with your own life, but I only need a little help. I promise I won't bother you too much."

Raven shook his head. "I don't care about that. Joel sent me here because he was worried you're training too much, yet you want to add more training to it?"

"A different training, not more of it. I'm sure you'll be able to tell me what I'm doing wrong, what I shouldn't be doing, and what I should be doing instead."

"I could, yes."

"Please?"

Turner bit his lower lip. He noticed Raven's gaze fluttering down to his mouth, then back up again to his eyes, and he wondered if Raven found him attractive. He'd never really thought about it.

Before, he hadn't wanted to be attractive to anyone because Alpha Rhodes was planning on selling him, and whoever found him attractive would buy him. After his rescue, he'd been busy healing and training. He'd never been in a relationship, but he found himself wondering how it would feel to kiss Raven. Would Raven even want that, or would he push Turner away? Turner didn't want to be rejected, but he also wanted to find out how Raven's lips felt. He suspected Raven would say no, anyway. He wouldn't put anything in jeopardy by kissing the man. It might be his only chance to be so close to someone, since Raven was one of the few people he trusted.

Raven looked like he was about to say no, so Turner stepped closer, quickly pressing his lips against Raven's. Just as quickly, he leaned back.

Raven stared. He hadn't reacted, but then Turner hadn't given him a chance to. It had all been too fast.

What the fuck?

Raven had no idea what had just happened, but he wanted Turner to kiss him again. That wasn't what he focused on, though.

"Did you kiss me to convince me to train you?" he asked.

Turner looked like Raven had just slapped him. "Of course not."

"Why did you do it, then?"

Turner looked away and shrugged. "Because I wanted to. I figured you were going to say no anyway, and I could have at least this. I apologize. I shouldn't have done it, because I know better than most people what it's like not to be able to say no."

Raven couldn't believe Turner was comparing the kiss they'd shared to what had been done to him. "That's not what this is about."

"Maybe not, but it should be. I'm sorry."

Raven was *so* confused. "I would have pushed you away if I didn't want you to kiss me. In fact, if I had things my way, you'd kiss me again and again."

Turner's eyes went wide. "Why?"

"Why not? You're attractive, and I like you."

"But you don't know me."

"Not well, no, but I know you enough to know that you're

strong and brave."

"I don't feel that way."

"How you feel doesn't matter. Everyone can see how strong you are." But, once again, they were getting side-tracked. "Why do you want me to train you, really?" Because there was no way Turner was telling the truth, at least not entirely.

Raven believed Turner never wanted to feel vulnerable again, but he'd already been training on his own. He might not know how to fight, but he wouldn't take anyone trying to hurt him without fighting back. He might not be lying, but Raven suspected there was more to it, and he wanted to know what it was.

He wasn't surprised when Turner shook his head and started to move away. "Never mind. It was stupid."

Raven grabbed his arm. It probably wasn't the smartest move, considering what Turner had gone through, but Raven needed to stop him. He let go as soon as Turner stopped moving, raising his hands to show him he wasn't dangerous.

Instead of freaking out like Raven had expected him to, Turner's shoulders slumped, and he turned to face him again. "Fine. I do want to be able to defend myself, but I'm also planning on killing Alpha Rhodes."

Raven gaped. His brain was stuck on the words, and he couldn't seem to think of a good way to answer. The only thing that came out of his mouth was, "You're planning on killing Alpha Rhodes?"

Turner raised his chin and crossed his arms over his chest. "You don't think I could do it?"

"I don't think you *should* do it. You can't go around killing people, Turner."

"I'm aware of that, and it's not what I'm doing."

"You just said that you're going to kill Alpha Rhodes."

"Only him. You know what he did, to me and to others.

You know he's going to do it again if we let him, and that's what's happening right now. The council isn't doing anything to stop him, and that's not right."

Raven understood how Turner felt. This was what he'd been telling Alex only a few days ago, so he truly did. But he couldn't let Turner do something so foolish.

"Look, I've never been through what you went through, but I do understand the need for revenge. I know why you want to kill him, and to be honest, I agree with the fact that someone should do something. That someone can't be you, though."

"Why not?"

"Because you can't just kill someone. If Alpha Rhodes is going to be taken care of, the council will have to do it."

Which was ironic, considering Alex had needed to say the same words to Raven only days ago. Raven hadn't been planning on killing Alpha Rhodes, but still.

Turner wasn't answering. Raven could tell by his expression that he hadn't given up, and he didn't know how to make him change his mind.

"You're free," he said, trying to appeal to Turner. "You can do whatever you want with your life. Why would you want to ruin it for that man?"

"You don't understand. I'm not ruining my life. I'm taking it back. This is what I need to do to be safe."

"You already *are* safe. You're with the cete, and the rest of the members, and I will make sure nothing happens to you."

"What if you can't? You can't be with me for the rest of my life, day in and day out. I have to be able to defend myself and make sure I'm safe. I'm the only one who can do that."

Raven was panicking. He didn't know how to get Turner to see he was doing the wrong thing. He wasn't even sure he could, but after everything Turner had told him, he needed to keep an eye on him and make sure he didn't do anything stupid.

"You should forget about Rhodes and focus on your future."

"How can I do that after what he did to me?"

"I understand it's not easy. I'm sorry about what happened to you, and the bastard should pay for what he did. He *will* pay, eventually. But you can't be the one to do it."

"Because I'm weak. Because this isn't my place. I'm a carrier, so I should be barefoot in the kitchen having children, right?"

"I never said that, and I don't believe it. You should be able to do everything you want to do."

"Except killing Alpha Rhodes."

"Yes, except that. No matter how much you train, it would take you years to know enough to be safe around him. If you try doing this anytime soon, *he'll* win, not you. Do you really want to risk that?"

"Yes!" Turner screamed. "And I won't let anyone stop me, not even you. If you don't want to train me, that's fine. I'll do it on my own."

Raven reached for Turner again, desperate to stop him. Before he could touch him, Turner shifted into his skunk form. That didn't stop Raven, and he grabbed Turner, holding him close to his chest.

Then, Turner did the unimaginable.

He glared at Raven and sprayed him.

It took only a second for Raven to drop Turner. It was a second too long, and Raven could already smell the stench clinging to his skin. He still made sure Turner hadn't hurt himself when he'd fallen to the ground, but Turner was gone. Raven saw the end of his tail disappearing between the trees, but even though he wanted to go after him, he stayed where he was.

Turner had made his decision, at least when it came to this.

He'd taken a risk, telling Raven what he was planning, but Raven didn't know what to do with that knowledge. Should he go to Thomas? He was tempted to do just that, but Turner would hate him if he did. On the other hand, Turner would do something stupid if Raven didn't do something.

He sniffed. Right now, the only thing he could do was go home and get rid of this stench. He doubted Turner was planning to do anything anytime soon. He was aware of the fact that he wasn't trained enough to face his old alpha, so hopefully, he wouldn't do anything stupid.

And if he did, well, Raven would be there to catch him. If Turner fell, Raven would put the pieces back together.

CHAPTER THREE

How many days would need to pass before Turner wasn't pissed about how his conversation with Raven had gone? Turner didn't know, but the anger was very much still alive in his chest, burning every time he thought about it.

He hadn't meant to spray Raven, but he'd acted on instinct when Raven had grabbed him. He'd known Raven wouldn't hurt him, but his brain hadn't seemed to remember that in the moment. Not that Turner cared. As far as he was concerned, Raven had gotten what he deserved. He should have known better than to grab Turner or try to change his mind.

Turner *wasn't* changing his mind. He'd kill Alpha Rhodes, and since no one was going to help him, he'd do it on his own. He might be a carrier, but he wasn't weak, and he'd show everyone who doubted him.

But how? He still didn't know how. He'd never killed anyone, and no matter how angry he was, he knew it wouldn't be easy. He couldn't count on his anger to carry him through it. It would be too easy for Alpha Rhodes to find a way around it. That meant that Turner would have to be good enough to sneak into skunk territory and into Alpha Rhodes's house, enter without anyone noticing him, get to him, and kill him.

Just the thought made his knees feel weak.

So yes, he was pissed, and he was taking it out on everyone around him. It made him feel guilty, but he didn't seem to be able to stop. That was why he'd been staying away from the other carriers at the Bishop house. He didn't want to hurt any of them, and he knew they were worried about him. If their roles were reversed, he'd be worried about them, too.

If any of them behaved the way Turner had been behaving recently, he'd demand an explanation. He was lucky none of them had yet, but that wouldn't last. Staying away from the house and everyone was easier, but unfortunately, Turner couldn't stay away forever. The Bishop house was his home, no matter how long he stayed away.

But it didn't solve his problems.

That was why he found himself standing in front of Kari's house.

Kari had been his only friend when Turner had been in the shed. He'd been the only person apart from Alpha Rhodes and a few people who had given him food that Turner had seen for weeks, possibly months. Kari had wanted to free Turner right away, but even Turner had known it would be a bad idea. So, instead of doing that, Kari had brought Turner food. He'd been a companion when Turner had believed he was entirely alone. He'd kept Turner sane, even when Turner had felt he was about to go nuts. Turner would have died without Kari, and he'd always be grateful to the man.

In any other situation, Turner would ask Kari to help him. Kari had learned how to fight on his own, and he was good. Even so, he hadn't been able to kill Alpha Rhodes, but he'd gotten rid of other alphas. There was no one Turner trusted more to train him.

The problem was that Kari had just given birth.

It wasn't *really* a problem. Turner didn't begrudge Kari for being happy and having found love. Kari had spent his entire life in the forest with only his father, and he deserved everything he was getting. He deserved to be happy, and he was. He was in love with a wonderful man and had a little boy. He should focus on them, not on Turner freaking out. This was a bad idea, and while Turner had known it would be from the beginning, it hadn't stopped him.

It did now.

He stared at the house for a moment, then started to turn away. But of course, the front door opened, and Kari stepped onto the porch. He was holding his son, and he looked so happy and at peace that Turner barely recognized him.

"What are you doing out here?" Kari asked.

"Nothing. I was just headed home."

Kari arched a brow. "Pity that the Bishop house isn't anywhere near here. Come in. I know you want to talk to me."

"I should leave you alone. I'm sure you have things to do."

"Like what? Changing diapers? You can do that for me. It'll give me a break."

"You want a break from your son?"

Kari glared. "You'd want a break, too, if you'd just had a baby. Believe me."

"I believe you."

And since Kari had ordered him to come in, Turner obeyed. He couldn't say no to Kari.

"I heard you sprayed someone," Kari said as soon as Turner was inside.

He also thrust his son into Turner's arms. Turner had no idea what to do with the baby, but he put his hand behind the baby's head and held him close to his chest. It felt odd and awkward, but he wasn't going to protest.

Kari led the way into his living room and flopped onto the couch with a heavy sigh. He closed his eyes, looking relaxed in a way Turner couldn't imagine being. Of course, Kari had never had an alpha. No one had ever threatened to sell him and almost succeeded.

"Well?" Kari asked after a moment. "What happened?"

"I shouldn't have sprayed Raven."

"Maybe, maybe not. What did he do?"

"I asked him if he could help me train. I don't ever want to feel weak again. I want to be able to defend myself if I see

Alpha Rhodes."

Kari nodded. "I get that."

Of course he did. He was still a carrier, no matter how he'd grown up. He, better than a lot of people, could understand why Turner felt this way.

"He didn't say no, but he seems to think I should focus on other things."

Kari snorted. "Like what? You won't be able to focus on anything else until you know you're safe, and the only way to make that happen is to be able to defend yourself."

Turner prayed that Raven hadn't told anyone about the other part of his plan. "Exactly. I don't think Raven can understand that, though."

"Probably not. He's never been in our shoes."

"And he never will be," Calder said as he walked in.

Thankfully, he took pity on Turner and took his son from Turner's arms after only a glance in his direction.

"I see you've already dumped the baby on someone else," he teased.

Kari glared at him. "Do I have to tell you what I went through to get the baby out of my body? I think I deserve to have someone wait on me hand and foot and to take care of the little monster while I recuperate."

Turner laughed. This was one more reason he enjoyed spending time with Kari. He might be a carrier, but people didn't treat him as if he were weak, even though he'd just had a baby. He'd shown everyone, including the council, that he was stronger than most of them. No one would ever doubt what he could do.

"I could help you train," Kari offered.

"That won't be possible," Calder intervened.

Kari glared at him. "And who are you to tell me that?"

"The man you love and the father of your child. Your body has just been through a lot, like you pointed out only seconds ago. You're not in any shape to train anyone."

Kari pouted. "Having a baby doesn't mean I can't do it."

"I know you want to help Turner, and I understand. Your body is not up to it, though, Kari. You'll end up hurting yourself, and I don't want that to happen."

Since Turner hadn't expected this to work, he wasn't disappointed. "It's fine. I understand you have to focus on your family."

"You should talk to Thomas," Kari suggested.

"Thomas?"

"He's the alpha. He'll provide you with everything you need, including someone to teach you how to fight."

"I don't think he'll want me to fight."

"Why not? If you ever want to be a guard for the cete or something like that, he'll make it happen. You just have to say the words."

Could it be so easy?

Turner hadn't thought about telling Thomas what he wanted to do. There was no way he was mentioning wanting to kill Alpha Rhodes, but as long as he didn't say anything about that, why would Thomas say no? Kari was right when he said that Thomas provided his people with everything they could want. No other carrier had wanted to learn to fight, but that didn't mean Thomas would disagree with Turner's request.

Once again, the only way for Turner to find out was to ask. He hoped things would go better this time.

"Hello?" Raven said.

"Raven," Thomas's voice boomed through the phone. "Do you think you can come to my office? I'd like to talk to you."

"Is there anything I should be worried about?"

Thomas chuckled. "Not unless you've done something you

shouldn't have."

"I haven't, as far as I remember."

"I'll be in my office when you get here."

Unfortunately, Thomas hadn't given Raven even a hint of what he could expect, so Raven was nervous the entire time he walked to Thomas's house.

Had Alex told him what Raven had done at the gym the other day? Surely Thomas wouldn't hold that against him. Everyone found Alastair irritating, not just Raven.

Or maybe it was Turner. Raven hadn't dared to go after him or visit him at the Bishop house since Turner had run away from him. A lot of people had teased him about getting sprayed, but he hadn't told anyone it had been Turner. He wasn't ashamed or anything like that, but he didn't want to direct more attention to Turner, especially with what Turner was planning.

Raven still thought it was stupid. There was no way Turner could kill Rhodes, and even if he could, he shouldn't. Raven understood why Turner was focused on that, but just wanting to was not a good enough reason to kill someone.

But what Turner had said about not being safe until Rhodes was gone made sense. That was why Rhodes should be arrested and locked up for the rest of his life. Would that be enough to stop Turner, though? For some reason, Raven didn't believe it would. That meant he'd have to keep an eye on Turner, and he wasn't sure how. He didn't want people to think he was a creeper, and he didn't want to freak out Turner even more.

When he got to the house, he walked right in. Thomas's wife was in the kitchen, but he didn't stop to chat with her like he would have any other day. Instead, he waved and walked right to the office, needing to know what was going on. He knocked, then, when Thomas told him to come in, opened the door.

And froze.

Turner was there, sitting in one of the chairs in front of Thomas's desk. He didn't look at Raven, but Raven could tell Turner was aware of his presence. His back was ramrod straight, and he stared ahead, quite obviously ignoring him.

Raven cleared his throat. "Yes?" he asked. Had Turner complained about him to Thomas? It hadn't sounded like it when Thomas had spoken to Raven on the phone, but something might have happened in the meantime.

"Sit down, sit down," Thomas said.

Raven obeyed, sitting on the edge of the chair. He didn't like not knowing what was going on, dammit.

"Turner came to me with a question, and I'd like to hear what you think about it," Thomas said.

"I'm listening," Raven told him. There was no way Turner had told Thomas he wanted to kill Rhodes. If he had, Thomas wouldn't be so calm.

"You know Turner, so you know his history."

"I was there when he was rescued," Raven confirmed.

"So it'll make sense to you, too, that he wants to learn how to defend himself. I understand that telling him he's safe here and that no one will hurt him doesn't make it so that he can feel safe, and besides, he might decide to move out. It's not a bad idea for Turner to be able to defend himself, and I'd like you to teach him self-defense."

So Turner *hadn't* told Thomas the truth. Raven looked at Turner and arched a brow when Turner made eye contact. Turner's cheeks flushed, but he held Raven's gaze as if daring him to say something.

Raven wouldn't. He still hoped he'd be able to change Turner's mind, at least when it came to killing Rhodes, but he didn't have a problem teaching Turner self-defense.

Still, Raven was tempted to tell Thomas about Turner's plans. That would be the best way to make sure Turner never did anything like that. Before going to Thomas with the information, though, he'd try talking to Turner again. Maybe spending time together would show Turner that Raven really only had his best interests at heart and that he didn't think Turner was weak in any way, shape, or form. Not wanting Turner to kill someone didn't have anything to do with strength or weakness. Raven just wanted to shield Turner from something that would hurt him for the rest of his life if he wasn't careful.

"Raven?" Thomas asked. He sounded puzzled, probably because Raven still hadn't answered. "I can find someone else if you're too busy or unable to do it."

"That won't be necessary. I'll be happy to teach Turner and anyone else who wants self-defense. You're right when you say they need to be able to defend themselves and feel like they'll never be a victim again. It's the least I can do."

Thomas looked satisfied, while Turner looked like he wanted to tear off Raven's face. He probably did, come to think of it.

"Perfect," Thomas said. His eyes twinkled with something Raven couldn't identify but which didn't bode well, although in what way, he didn't know yet. "The two of you should start talking about when and where you'll train."

"I thought the gym would be the perfect place," Raven offered. "It's already set up for this kind of thing."

"Of course. Just, please make sure it doesn't interfere with everyone else's training."

"I will."

And he'd make sure Turner knew what he thought about his plans and that he'd do everything he could to stop him if talking to him wasn't enough. He didn't want to hurt Turner, and he wouldn't, but if he had to, he'd go to Thomas and explain what was going on. There was no way this situation would end well if he let Turner do what he was planning.

Raven had always been a protector, although until recently, he'd only protected the cete. Now, he felt the need to do the same for Turner and to protect him from himself. Hopefully it wouldn't come to that, but if it did, Raven would do what he had to do, even if it meant Turner hated him by the time this was over. It would be worth it if it meant Turner was safe.

Turner wanted to yell that he'd changed his mind, but he couldn't without looking like an asshole. He'd asked Thomas to find someone to help him train and learn to fight, and Thomas had. It wasn't his fault he didn't know something was going on between Raven and Turner—whatever that was.

He hadn't talked to Raven since he'd sprayed him, and he hadn't believed he would. He'd been terrified Raven would tell someone about his plans for Alpha Rhodes, but so far, he didn't think Raven had. Still, he kept expecting him to do it, especially now that Thomas was asking him to step in officially.

So far, Raven was keeping his mouth shut. If anything, he'd seemed open to helping, which Turner didn't understand and expected came with conditions. Even if it did, he wasn't giving up his plan. He might not know what he was doing just yet, but that would change, and he'd kill Alpha Rhodes.

Turner didn't even care what happened to him after he did. He realized he'd probably be incarcerated, as would be right. Kari hadn't been arrested after killing an alpha, but no one had been able to prove he'd done it. He was too good, but Turner wasn't. He had no doubt someone would find out he'd been the one to kill Alpha Rhodes.

But thinking about this might be pointless. It meant Turner believed he had a chance to make it out of this alive, and he wasn't sure he did. What were the odds that he'd manage to kill his old alpha without a scratch? Not many, and he didn't expect it to happen. But even if Alpha Rhodes ended up killing him, Turner wouldn't back down. He couldn't afford to, no matter what Raven believed.

Thomas clapped his hands, possibly to get Turner's attention. "All right. Well, since this has been settled, I think the two of you should have a chat. You don't really know each other, and you should."

Turner was afraid to look in Raven's direction. What would he see if he did?

"We should," Raven confirmed. "And you're probably right that we should at least have a chat before we start training. I wouldn't want Turner to react badly."

That got Turner glaring at him. "What do you mean?"

"Well, with what you've been through, I don't want you to think I'm going to hurt you when I teach you to fight. I mean, it's obvious I'll need to touch you, possibly punch you. I'd rather not terrify you as I do so."

"I'm not so weak that I don't understand this is necessary to get what I want," Turner said through gritted teeth.

"That's not what Raven said," Thomas gently scolded. "He's only thinking about your well-being. He's not wrong that you've been through a lot, and he's worried he's going to make things worse instead of better."

"I'll be fine."

"I'm sure you will, or, at the very least, that it's what you want to believe."

From anyone else, it would have sounded patronizing. Coming from Thomas, Turner knew it was because he cared. Thomas didn't want Turner or anyone else to be hurt, which was why Turner had been surprised he'd agreed with his request so readily.

Turner sucked in a breath, not wanting to snap at the alpha.

"I understand your concerns, and I'm grateful for them. I know you care about my well-being, and I'm grateful for that, too. I suppose it's just hard to get used to. My old alpha didn't exactly worry about me or how I was."

Thomas scowled. "That man should never have become an alpha, and he shouldn't be one right now."

"I agree." And Turner would do something about it.

"Good. Now, I really have work to do. I'd love to chat with the two of you soon, though. I want to know how you're doing, Turner."

"I'll come by in a few weeks when you're not as busy."

"Come around sooner. We'd love to have you for dinner. You, too, Raven."

Raven smiled and gave a ridiculous little bow. It made Thomas laugh, and Turner looked from one to the other.

Every time he'd seen Raven, the man had been serious. He'd struck Turner as someone who didn't laugh often, yet here he was, having fun with Thomas. Maybe Turner didn't know Raven as well as he'd assumed. That wasn't surprising, considering how little they'd talked.

He left the office, intent on running back to the Bishop house. He might have to talk to Raven soon, but that didn't mean he had to do it now. Turner couldn't help but wonder why Raven hadn't told Thomas what he was planning on doing with the training he'd provide. He was grateful, but he didn't like feeling like he owed Raven anything.

Turner would ask Raven why he'd agreed to train him, but not now.

Turner made his way to the front door, but, before he could reach it, Joel appeared. He beamed at Turner, making Turner internally cringe. He loved Joel, he really did, but the man was a lot on the best of days, and right now, Turner didn't feel this was a good day.

"Turner! I didn't know you were here," Joel said.

"I had to talk to your father," Turner said curtly, hoping Joel would understand from his tone of voice that he wasn't here to have a chat.

Joel either didn't understand or didn't care, because he grabbed Turner's arm and pulled him in the direction of the kitchen. "What did you have to talk to him about?"

"Something." Joel was worried that Turner was training too much, so he probably wouldn't appreciate him going to his father to demand more training.

"That doesn't tell me what the two of you talked about," he said, punctuating his words with a pout.

They walked into the kitchen, where Joel's mother was cooking. She smiled at them, and Turner found himself smiling back.

She reminded him of his mother, back before Turner had discovered he was a carrier. They used to cook together and generally spent time in the kitchen, and he missed it. He missed his mother, or at least, the mother she'd been before she'd had to hand him over to Alpha Rhodes.

"You boys want a snack?" she asked.

Turner wanted to point out neither of them were boys, but Joel was already nodding. "Please. Did you bake cookies?"

"You know there are always cookies in the kitchen." She grabbed the ceramic container from the counter and settled it onto the table. "Sit down. I'll grab the two of you some milk, or maybe you want something else?"

"Milk is fine," Turner murmured as he obeyed her order. She wasn't the alpha, but she was the alpha mate, and he was supposed to obey her. Not that she'd ever say anything about anyone disobeying her, but still.

"So, what have you been up to?" Joel asked.

Turner desperately wanted out of this conversation, but he liked Joel and his mother. He couldn't just leave, no matter how tempted he was.

"Nothing much," he ended up saying.

"For some reason, I'm pretty sure that's a lie, but fine. You're not up to anything."

"I'm not." Turner hesitated. Joel was going to find out about this sooner rather than later anyway. He might as well tell him. "I talked to your father about finding someone who could train me."

Joel frowned. "I thought you'd decided against that."

"I haven't. I feel I need this to be able to think about my future rather than my past, and your father agreed. He asked Raven to train me."

Joel's eyes widened. "Even though you sprayed him?"

Turner groaned. "Does everyone know about that?"

"Pretty much. You know how the cete is. We all know everything that happens around here. Did you expect no one would talk about it?"

"I guess I had hoped it wouldn't be such a big deal."

"It's not every day someone sprays Raven."

"I shouldn't have. I guess I panicked."

Joel frowned. "Why? Did he do something to scare you?"

"He wouldn't. We were just talking, and I got angry at something he said. I shifted and tried running away, and he tried to apologize and grabbed me. I sprayed him. I swear to you he didn't do anything he shouldn't have. It was an over-reaction on my part."

Joel didn't look convinced, but Turner hoped he wouldn't push. He didn't want to continue talking about this.

He didn't want to continue talking about anything, and he smiled gratefully when Joel's mother set two glasses and a bottle of milk on the table. Thankfully, it was enough to distract Joel, and the conversation shifted to something else.

Turner leaned back in his chair, relieved. He didn't want to lie to Joel, so it was better if Joel stopped asking questions.

He had, at least for now.

Raven had wanted to go after Turner and ask him what was going on, but before he could, Thomas stopped him.

"Raven?" Thomas said before Raven could leave the office.

Whatever he was about to say, Raven doubted he'd like it. Still, he stopped. "Yes?"

"I know what Turner is up to."

That was enough to make Raven freeze. "You do?"

"I wasn't born yesterday. I'm not an idiot, and I know what I'd want to do if I were in Turner's place."

"But you wouldn't do it."

Thomas gestured at Raven to close the door. Raven obeyed, wondering where the conversation would go. Maybe he shouldn't have been surprised that Thomas knew. He seemed to know everything that happened in their territory, and he'd always been good at reading people.

Raven settled back into his chair once the door was closed, facing his alpha. Thomas was lost in his thoughts, but he shook himself. "You're right. I wouldn't kill him, or at least, I like to think I wouldn't. I'm not in Turner's position, though, and I never was. Neither were you, for that matter."

"I might not know what he's been through in detail, but you and I both know this isn't a good idea."

"I agree. I doubt Turner will even be able to hurt Rhodes, no matter how hard he tries. And I don't like the thought of sending him there and having Rhodes possibly hurt him. That's what's going to happen if we don't intervene, though."

"Yet you agreed to have me train him."

"You know what he'd have done if I'd said no. He's already been doing it."

"Is that how you found out?"

"Turner is hurting," Thomas said. "Everyone here knows that and can see it. He doesn't know what to do with his life now that he's free, or even how to be free, to begin with. Add to that the fact that Rhodes is still around, possibly hurting other carriers, and it makes sense that Turner wants to do something about it. He probably hopes that once Rhodes is gone, he'll finally be able to do what he wants with his life, and he doesn't realize he could do that already."

"I agree. I'm just not sure how to show him that."

"I don't think it's your job to do that. But if I'd said no, he'd have done this on his own, and something bad would have happened. Something is going to break eventually, and I'm afraid it's going to be Turner. That's why I asked you to do this with him. There's no one I trust more than you to help Turner."

"I'm not sure why you feel that way."

"How can I not? You're one of the best people I know. Turner is lost. He doesn't know what to do with himself, and that's not going to get better until he gets what he wants, or at least, what he thinks he wants. I want you to keep an eye on him. Someone needs to be there for him, someone he can rely on."

"And you think that's me."

"I'm sure it is. Turner might not realize it yet, but he needs you."

Turner wasn't going to be happy to hear that. "I hope you're right. I do want to help him, but I'm not sure anyone can at this point."

"Let's hope you're wrong."

"What if I'm not the right person?"

"I have faith in you."

Raven sat back. He knew Thomas was telling the truth, but it was still strange to hear. He didn't consider himself an asshole or anything like that, but how could Thomas have so much faith in him when he didn't have it in himself?

"But be careful not to mother him too much," Thomas

51

added. "That would be counterproductive, and that's not what we want."

"I'll do what I can."

"I know. You'll do your best, like always. That's why I'm asking you, of all people, to do it. I'd trust you with my life, and I trust you with Turner's."

Raven's mind was still reeling by the time he left the office. He might not understand why Thomas was choosing him, but he didn't have to. Thomas was his alpha, and Raven would obey his orders. In this case, Thomas wanted him to take care of Turner, so that was what Raven would do. He might not be sure he could do a good job, but he was certainly going to try.

Raven walked to the front door, but he heard voices coming from the kitchen before he could reach it. He recognized Turner's, and he had to resist the urge to peek inside, maybe stop and talk to him.

He was sure Turner didn't want to see him right now. He'd gone to Thomas for help, and he'd gotten it, but there was no way he'd wanted or expected Raven to be that help. It would take him a while to wrap his mind around it and accept it, and during that time, Raven would stay away. He'd wait for Turner to come to him instead. He would have to eventually, if he wished to start training, and when he did, Raven would lay down the law.

If they were going to work together, they'd have rules, and Turner would have to follow them. Otherwise, he'd be on his own trying to kill his old alpha.

Raven hoped things wouldn't come to that.

Chapter Four

Turner still didn't want to train with Raven, but he'd eventually contacted the man since there wasn't a way out of it. They'd agreed to see each other today at the gym, and Turner was excited, wary, and nervous.

He couldn't help but wonder if Raven was going to say something about what Turner was planning and if maybe he'd try to stop him. Turner wouldn't be surprised, but he'd come to realize that Raven wasn't the person he thought he was. It would have been easy for him to go straight to Thomas, especially when Turner had asked the alpha for help, but Raven hadn't. He'd kept Turner's secret, and while Turner didn't understand why, he was grateful. The problem was that it made him feel like Raven had some kind of power over him, and that wasn't something he ever wanted anyone to have again.

Turner realized it was stupid. Thomas was his new alpha, and as such, he had power over him. Just like Thomas, Raven was a good person. He wouldn't use what he knew against Turner, but unfortunately, that didn't help Turner feel better. He really wished he could forget all of this and focus on the day, but not knowing what was about to happen and what Raven's plan was made him nervous.

He'd arrived early, wanting to look around before Raven got there. Unfortunately for him, he wasn't the only one who had that thought, and when he walked into the gym, he saw that Raven was already on the mats. He didn't seem to have heard Turner, and Turner took the opportunity to take him in.

He was wearing a pair of shorts and nothing else. Was that how training usually went? Turner couldn't say he'd ever given a lot of attention to what was going on around him while he trained in the gym, but he was pretty sure everyone had been wearing shirts. He didn't understand why Raven wasn't, but he supposed it was none of his business. As long as Raven did what they were here to do, he didn't care how he was dressed. He could be naked, for all Turner cared.

All right, maybe that wasn't true. Turner *would* have a problem if Raven was naked, if anything because he wouldn't be able to stop staring. Raven was distracting enough as it was without a shirt on.

Turner was still staring when Raven turned around, aiming a kick high. He didn't freeze when he saw Turner. Instead, he finished the movement before putting both of his feet back on the floor and finally turning to face him.

"I wasn't sure you'd come," he said.

Turner narrowed his eyes. "Why wouldn't I? I'm the one who wants to train. Actually, I'm surprised *you* came. Is it only because your alpha ordered you to?"

Raven glared. "This is a stupid idea, and I made sure Thomas knew that."

The bottom of Turner's stomach dropped. "What did you tell him?"

"Are you asking if I told him about your little plan?"

"Yes." It was no use to dance around the issue. "Did you, then?"

Raven's shoulders relaxed just a tiny bit. "Of course I didn't. Do you really think I'm that kind of person?"

"I don't know what kind of person you are. I barely know you."

"Yet you told me what you were planning. Why?"

Turner couldn't tell him it was because even though they

barely knew each other, he trusted him. "It was a stupid thing to do, but it's too late now, I guess."

Raven stared for a moment before shaking his head. "I don't understand you."

"I don't care. As long as you're here and train me, you don't have to understand me or even like me."

"Why are you so hell-bent on this? I understand you want revenge and to make sure Rhodes doesn't hurt anyone again but is this really the right way to do that?"

"It's the only way I know how to do it. Now, are we here to fight, or are we here to talk?"

Raven sighed, but thankfully, he didn't say anything else. Instead, he gestured at Turner to step onto the mat. Turner had already been through this, so he knew what to do. He took off his shoes, leaving them next to the mat. He wasn't about to take his t-shirt off, though, so he was already done. He went to stand in front of Raven, wondering what was about to happen.

There was no way Raven wasn't pissed about the spraying, at the very least. Turner couldn't know whether or not he'd take it out on him, but he hoped the answer was no. He wouldn't be able to do anything to defend himself, and the last thing he needed was for Raven to pound him into the mats.

But Turner was here to learn, and learn he would, even if he got hurt in the process. He fully expected he would be.

"Now," Raven started. "Do you know anything about fighting?"

"Not really. You're going to have to start from the beginning."

To his surprise, Raven didn't look angry. "That's what I expected. Are you ready?"

"As ready as I'll ever be." Hopefully, Raven wouldn't take his anger out on Turner.

"This isn't going to be easy, and it's not going to be nice," Raven warned.

Turner squared his shoulders. "I'm ready."

He really wasn't. After only a few minutes, he regretted all of his life decisions. Raven had already slammed him into the mats five times—not that Turner was counting. Obviously, Raven tried to do it lightly so Turner wouldn't get hurt too badly, but it didn't work. Turner felt every single hit of Raven's hands on his arms, stomach, and thighs. Desperation was crowding him, telling him he didn't know what he was doing and that he'd never be able to do it, but he pushed it away.

He *could* do this. He didn't care how many times he fell and how much pain he was in. He wasn't changing his mind. He'd show everyone in the forest, including Raven and Alpha Rhodes, that he was strong.

Raven was surprised that Turner wasn't giving up already. He'd decided not to go easy on him, and he wasn't. Yet Turner still stood up every time he fell to the mats. He was incredible, but Raven didn't say it. He still thought Turner shouldn't be doing this, and he wanted Turner to remember that.

Once again, Turner got back to his feet. He had a bruise already forming on the corner of his jaw where Raven had caught him earlier. Raven hadn't meant to do it, but Turner had tried to avoid his punch to the shoulder, and Raven had caught his jaw instead.

"Again," Turner said.

Raven shook his head. "You're only getting hurt."

"I don't care." Turner raised his fists. "I'm ready."

"Turner, you don't know what you're getting yourself into. You're going to be in trouble—if you don't get hurt, or worse, killed. Is that really what you want?"

"I can do this," Turner said through gritted teeth.

"You can't even handle this training. How do you expect to be able to fight and kill Rhodes?"

"I'll get better."

"It'll take you years." And somehow, Raven doubted Turner would want to wait that long to get back at Rhodes.

"Again," Turner said.

Since he wasn't backing down, Raven would show him what he was going against.

Raven was a guard, and he was trained as such. He doubted Rhodes had the same training, especially since the man seemed to think nothing and no one could touch him, but still. It was better to be over-prepared, and if Turner couldn't take Raven on, he had no hope against Rhodes. Raven needed him to understand how bad things could get, and since the only way to make that happen was to hurt Turner, he would. It was better than sending Turner into the lion's den on his own.

So Raven obeyed Turner's request. He jerked to the side, and, as he'd expected, Turner followed the movement. Raven used that advantage to strike on the other side, clipping Turner on the flank, then, when Turner folded in on himself, on the shoulder. At the same time, he swiped his leg against Turner's, and Turner fell to the mat.

This time, Turner didn't get up. Raven waited, sure Turner would have something to say about what he'd just done. Instead, Turner was barely moving. The only sound in the room was Turner's breathing, and when Raven moved closer, he saw a fine trace of blood on Turner's cheek. It wasn't much, and nothing Raven would have freaked out over if he'd been in Turner's place, but he wasn't.

"What the fuck do you think you're doing?" a voice boomed behind Raven.

Raven turned and found Jacob striding toward them, looking pissed.

"I told you Thomas asked me to do this," Raven said.

"To train him, sure. Not to pound him into the mats."

"He wants this."

But Jacob wasn't having any of it. He grabbed Raven's arm and towed him toward the door, no doubt to yell at him in private. For once, though, none of this was Raven's fault. He didn't want to do this anymore than Jacob wanted him to, but what was he supposed to do?

Jacob dragged Raven outside. Raven tried to go back in, and when Jacob stopped him, he protested. "I have to check in on him."

"And you will after I'm done yelling at you. He's fine, just tired, probably angry, and in pain." He put his hands on his hips. "What are you doing?"

Raven crossed his arms over his chest. "What Turner and Thomas asked me to do."

"I don't think that's what Thomas intended."

But it was what Turner had wanted. Still, Raven should have known better than to try giving him that.

He swallowed. "I know I went hard on him, but I have to." Raven couldn't tell him what Turner was plotting. He didn't want his best friend to think badly of him, though.

"You don't *have* to do anything," Jacob protested. "He's not one of us. He can't stand this kind of training."

"I'm only doing what he wants and what Thomas asked me to do. Please, Jacob," Raven begged. "I can't tell you everything, but Turner would notice if I didn't treat him like everyone else, and he'd be pissed. He'd be right to, too. He's not fragile, and I shouldn't treat him with kid gloves. If I don't do this, he'll find someone else, and is there anyone you'd trust with him as much as you trust me? There's a reason Thomas asked *me* of all people to do this."

Jacob's glare had softened, but he still looked angry. "Why don't you tell me everything? How can I understand when I don't know the entire story?"

"It's not my secret to tell. And trust me. I wish I could have someone intervene. I can't, though."

"Because you don't want to."

"Because I can't betray him. He doesn't trust anyone, probably not even himself most of the time. I don't trust anyone else with this. I just don't want you to hate me by the time this is over."

Jacob sighed. "I don't hate you. I could *never* hate you. I'm just not sure what's going on, and I don't like it."

"Trust me. I like it as little as you do. But this is the only way this entire situation won't be a disaster."

Jacob stared for a moment before finally nodding. "Fine. I want to shout at Thomas about the situation, but I truly hope the two of you know what you're doing."

"We don't, but this is the only thing we can do about it."

"I don't want anyone to get hurt, but especially not one of the carriers."

"I understand where you're coming from and why you feel that way, but I don't think it's doing any of them any good to be treated differently. They're not fragile little toys to be put on a shelf. It's good that Thomas has given them a safe place to live where they can be themselves and where they don't have to be afraid of the rest of the world, but there's such a thing as protecting someone too much."

The corner of Jacobs's lips quirked. "I am very much aware that carriers aren't weak or fragile. And maybe you're right. Maybe after seeing and knowing what they've been through, everyone has been overprotective. It might be time to stop, but you have to understand how hard it can be for some of us."

Raven snorted. "I think it's hard for everyone. Do you

really think I want to beat Turner the way I have? But I do it because I know that not doing it would make everything worse."

Jacob clasped Raven's shoulder and squeezed. "You're lucky I trust you, because if I didn't, I would have beaten you into the mats when I saw what you were doing."

Raven batted his best friend's hand away. "You could have tried, but we both know you wouldn't have succeeded."

Jacob laughed, telling Raven they were okay. The problem was that Raven didn't know if he and Turner were, and for some reason, that was important to him. He didn't want Turner to be angry at him.

The problem was that Turner seemed to be angry at pretty much everything and everyone.

Turner was pissed. He'd known this wouldn't be easy, but how could he already be giving up?

His entire body hurt, and he needed a moment to breathe and gather himself. He wasn't giving up, and he hoped Raven knew that. Still, he was relieved that Jacob had dragged Raven outside, even though he was also miffed at the fact that Jacob seemed to believe he should protect him.

Turner didn't need anyone to protect him.

He got into a sitting position and rubbed his forearm over his face, attempting to get the sweat off. His cheek burned, and when he touched it, his fingers came away slightly bloody. He shrugged and used his t-shirt to get rid of the blood. He had no idea how he'd gotten hurt, and he didn't care.

"Let me help you," a man said.

Turner hadn't heard him walk in, too busy pouting. The man was right next to the mats, and he reached for Turner.

"I don't need your help," Turner snapped, glaring at the

man.

The man's eyes widened, and he stepped back, raising his hands. "Sorry I asked. Everyone needs help getting up once Raven's done with them, though."

Turner kept his focus on the man and struggled back to his feet. Every single muscle in his body felt weak, but he wouldn't show anyone that, least of all Raven, who was walking back toward them.

Now that Turner was looking around, he could see the gym was half full. Several people were watching, including the guy who'd tried to help him. And Calder, who was running on a treadmill, frowning at him. No matter how much Turner didn't want to, he turned his attention back to Raven, who'd reached him.

"Alastair," Raven said, his voice hard. "Are you giving Turner trouble?"

Alastair shook his head. He looked slightly panicked, which, after what he'd said about Raven, made sense. "I just wanted to help him. You went pretty hard on him."

Raven's glare deepened. "I didn't do anything he didn't want me to do."

"I never said you did. Sorry."

Alastair walked away, keeping an eye on Raven as if he expected him to attack. It was ridiculous, but Turner understood the feeling.

"Training is over for the day," Raven said.

Turner frowned. "I can take more."

"I don't care what you can take. Go home and rest." His expression softened. "I'm not saying this because I think you're weak. I'm saying it because it won't do you and your body any good if you push yourself too hard. Trust me. I've been in this situation, and I understand wanting to continue until you finally get what you want. It's not going to happen today, though. Go home, take a warm bath, and rest. I'll see you tomorrow morning, same time."

Turner could tell he wouldn't change Raven's mind, so he stopped trying. He slowly walked toward the showers, wondering how he was supposed to get to the Bishop house when every single muscle hurt. He supposed he was going to find out.

"Turner?"

Turner almost groaned. "Yes?" he asked as he turned to face Calder.

Calder was off the treadmill, drying his face with a towel and still looking worried. "What's going on?"

"Nothing. You knew I wanted someone to teach me how to fight."

"Not like this, though. Are you hurt?"

"It's just a bruise."

"Bruises don't generally bleed," Calder pointed out.

"I'll be fine." Maybe if Turner repeated it often enough, Calder would believe it. Maybe Turner would end up believing it, too.

Calder hesitated. "I just want you to remember that if you need anything, Kari and I are here for you. I know you're probably not entirely comfortable with me, and I understand that. But Kari would kick my ass if I didn't do everything I could to make you comfortable. That includes offering you our guest room if you want to move out of the Bishop house and any help you might need to move on with your life."

Turner found himself smiling. "You just want someone to take care of the baby during the night."

Calder laughed. "I don't think Kari would mind, even though I'm usually the one who does nightly feedings." His smile softened. "I just want you to know we're all here for you."

"I know." And knowing that made Turner feel even more guilty.

The entire cete, but especially his friends, had been there for him since he'd arrived. They'd made sure he was safe, had food and clothes and everything he could ever want. How was he thanking them? By planning to kill Alpha Rhodes.

But he wasn't giving up. He couldn't, because he knew all too well how much harm Alpha Rhodes could do.

"Why are you still here?" Raven asked from behind Turner.

Turner glared at him. "I was talking with my friend. Can I, or am I too weak even for that?"

"I told you to go home, Turner. Are you trying to convince Calder to train with you?"

"Gosh, I hate you so much," Turner snapped. "I don't think you'll ever see me as anything but the guy you found in that shed, and I wish I could never see you again."

With that, Turner walked away. He didn't want to see Raven's reaction to his words. He didn't even care how Raven felt. At the moment, he truly hated the other man, and he was afraid of what that emotion would make him do. He wasn't about to attack Raven, not after Raven had shown him how easy it was for him to kick his ass, but he felt like he was about to explode. It was better for him to step away while he was able. He'd regret whatever he'd say next, and he needed Raven too much to piss him off even more.

For now, it was better if Turner did as Raven had ordered and walked away.

Raven watched Turner leave, making his chest feel tight. Why had it hurt so much when Turner told him he hated him? Raven didn't know Turner enough to be hurt by how he felt. Even though he'd been there when Turner had been rescued, that didn't mean they were friends. Besides, he suspected Turner didn't actually hate him. He'd had a rough day, and

Raven had been fussing over him in a way he shouldn't have.

Turner was fiercely independent, maybe too much. He didn't want anyone taking care of him for anything, which apparently included telling him to go home and rest after they'd trained.

"It could have been worse," Calder said from beside Raven.

Raven glared at him. "Really?"

"He didn't try to hit you."

Raven shook his head. "I should go after him."

"No, you shouldn't."

Calder's words were enough for Raven to stop. Calder wasn't the alpha, but he was the cete's council member. He held a lot of authority, and as a guard, Raven found himself obeying.

Calder smiled at him. "Give him time. He had all these plans of becoming strong and everything, then one morning with you, and he spent most of his time on his back on the mats. You have to see this from his point of view. He hoped things would go better, and since they haven't, he's taken it badly."

"This was a bad idea," Raven muttered.

"Maybe, maybe not. You'll find out in the next few days. In the meantime, let him come to you. Give him time to think over what happened today, how he reacted, and what you did. I'm sure that eventually he's going to realize you meant well."

"I'm not sure that will be the case."

"Well, if it's not, he'll have to give up his dream of becoming a guard, or whatever the reason is that he's doing this."

Turner wasn't doing it to become a guard, but Raven had told himself he'd keep Turner's promise, and he had every intention of doing just that. Calder didn't need to know what Turner was planning, not yet. Hopefully, Raven would manage to change Turner's mind. If he couldn't, he'd work with Thomas to get Turner to see how dangerous this was.

Since he couldn't go after Turner, Raven took out his phone. He had Turner's phone number because Thomas had insisted that they exchange numbers, and he brought it up. He quickly typed in a text.

Next training session is tomorrow morning.

Raven didn't add anything. If Turner wanted to be there, he would be. If he didn't, well, it wouldn't be a bad thing as far as Raven was concerned.

He put his phone away, wondering if Turner would come. Raven had been surprised to see him this morning, but he shouldn't have. Turner was convinced about what he was doing, and he wasn't allowing anyone or anything to stop him.

Or was that the case? What would he do next? Would he spend the rest of today pouting and be here tomorrow morning, or were the training sessions over?

Raven didn't know, but he'd find out soon enough.

He headed for the showers. Since Thomas had known they were doing this, he'd told Raven to take the rest of the day off, which Raven had been more than happy to do. He'd thought he and Turner could spend the day together, maybe get to know each other, but that had been a bust. Now, Raven didn't have anything to do but go home to his empty house, and he wasn't looking forward to it.

He loved his home, and he loved the cete, but sometimes, he wanted more. He wasn't sure when he'd started imagining Turner living with him and sharing his home, but he needed to forget it. Even if Turner did like him — which he wasn't convinced of — with everything that had happened between them, there was no way Turner would ever see him in that light.

To Turner, Raven was the asshole who knew his secret and who had pounded him into the mats this morning. He was the man who'd insist Turner continued training no matter what because it was the only way to keep an eye on him and know what he was doing.

And that was what mattered. Turner might be convinced about what he was doing, but Raven knew how bad an idea it was, and he'd keep Turner safe, whether or not Turner was happy about it.

Everyone needed help sometimes, and everyone needed someone by their side. It wasn't a sign of weakness, and Raven wasn't doing this because he thought Turner was weak. He was doing it because he cared, even though he didn't understand why or when it had happened. Maybe Turner couldn't see that, and maybe he never would, but it didn't matter. Nothing mattered but keeping Turner safe, and Raven was the best man for the job.

CHAPTER FIVE

Turner didn't want to be here, but he also didn't want Raven to win, which was why he was at the gym early once again.

He didn't know what to expect. The text he'd received from Raven yesterday after storming out had surprised him, but maybe it shouldn't have. Even though Raven was rough and had been hard on Turner, he cared. Turner was sure of that, even though he didn't understand why Raven felt that way.

It would have been easy to stay home, maybe text Raven he wasn't coming because he wasn't feeling well. After yesterday, no one would have been surprised. But Turner wasn't giving up. If he were, he'd have done it a while ago. Instead, he was here this morning, already on the mats, waiting for Raven. He'd been surprised to see the gym was empty when he'd arrived, and he was starting to wonder if Raven would turn up. Maybe he thought that Turner wouldn't come and that he shouldn't bother. If that was the case, Turner would make sure Raven knew what he thought about that. They had a deal, and Raven needed to respect it.

So here Turner was, wondering what was next for him. What would he do if Raven didn't come? Would he try to find someone else to help him train, or should he just give up? Should he go to Thomas and complain?

The sound of a door closing in the distance made Turner tense. He kept his focus on the door that led to the changing rooms, wondering who was there. He really hoped it was Raven, because he didn't know what he'd do if it was someone else. He didn't want to talk to anyone, not after what had happened yesterday. He wouldn't say he'd been humiliated, but it wasn't far from it.

Thankfully, when the door opened, it *was* Raven who walked in. Turner almost smiled because he was so relieved, but then he remembered what had happened yesterday and how they'd left each other.

He didn't know if he was still angry. He realized Raven hadn't been trying to coddle him, and he hadn't been telling him he was weak. He'd just been worried, and Turner needed to start accepting that a lot of people were worried about him. It wasn't just because he was a carrier and he'd almost been sold by his alpha. It was because these people cared about him as a person. He was their friend, no matter how hard it was to remember that or to accept it fully. They wanted him to be safe and happy, and they'd do everything they could to make that happen.

That was why Raven had insisted that Turner get some rest. It wasn't because he thought Turner was weak but because Turner had trained and his body wasn't used to what he and Raven had been doing.

Raven didn't look surprised when he saw Turner on the mats. He nodded curtly and came to stand in front of him, staring until Turner wanted to shuffle his feet. He wouldn't show Raven how uncomfortable he was, though, so instead, he raised his chin high and looked right at him.

For a moment, Raven stared back. Then, he nodded. "Good. Are you ready to start?"

"I've never been more ready for anything."

The corners of Raven's lips twitched. Turner wanted to ask him why he was amused, but he decided to focus on their training instead. "What will it be today?" he asked. "How many times will you punch me?"

Raven cracked his knuckles. "As many times as I have to

for you to learn how to do this."

Raven was more distant today, and Turner didn't blame him. How could he after what he'd said yesterday? He wanted to apologize and opened his mouth to do just that, but Raven was already moving toward him, and Turner had to defend himself.

For what felt like the next six hours, that was the only thing Turner could focus on. It was as if Raven was coming at him from every angle and every side, and he knew exactly where to strike. He probably did. This was his job, and he'd been trained to see the weaknesses in his adversaries and use them.

He didn't seem to have a problem doing just that with Turner.

Turner spent a lot of time on his back on the mat, and by the time Raven stopped moving, Turner was out of breath and hurting all over. It wasn't anything he hadn't expected, but he found that he missed the easy way he and Raven had talked yesterday.

Perhaps calling it easy wasn't the right word, but it had been nicer than today. Even though it was entirely his fault, Turner missed the old Raven. He wanted him back, but how? The best way would be to apologize, but Turner was afraid. What if Raven didn't accept his apology? What if he continued acting this way, and they never were friendly again?

Turner wasn't sure he could continue training with Raven when Raven barely spoke to him or looked at him.

"I think that's enough for today," Raven said with a grunt.

Once again, Turner was flat on the mats, staring at the ceiling. His arms were so sweaty they clung to the material, which made him wince when he wiggled.

He expected Raven to offer him a hand to help him to his feet, but instead, Raven had already turned and was moving away. Turner panicked and scrambled to his feet, needing to stop Raven. "Wait!"

Raven froze. "Yes?"

"Thank you."

Raven stared at Turner for a moment. "What are you thanking me for?"

"Helping me. I know you could have said no, but you didn't."

"I should have."

"You disagree with what I'm planning."

Raven snorted. "Disagree is an understatement. I think it's the stupidest idea I've ever heard, and I wish you'd listen to me when I say you shouldn't do it."

Turner ignored that, eager to change the topic of their conversation. "I wanted to apologize for how I behaved yesterday and to thank you." Turner didn't want to talk about Alpha Rhodes again. He wouldn't change his mind, and neither would Raven. He just wanted Raven back the way they'd been before Turner pitched a fit. They hadn't exactly been comfortable, but it had been better than today.

Raven stared at Turner for a moment longer before nodding and turning away again. This time, Turner didn't try to stop him. He could too easily imagine how Raven would react if he did, and he didn't think he could stand the heartache.

When had Raven become so important to Turner? And more importantly, *why*? Was it only because Raven had been the one to bring Turner out of that shed? Or was there more to it, and was Turner refusing to see it? Turner didn't know, but he did know he should start thinking about it.

He had no idea what his future would be like once he killed Alpha Rhodes, or even if he'd have one. But over the past few days, he'd found himself wondering if Raven would be a part of it. He'd been surprised to realize he wanted him to be, but he didn't know how to ask. Could he? There was nothing between him and Raven, and after what had happened, he doubted there ever would be.

And if there would, now wasn't the time to think about it. Turner had to focus on training and taking out Alpha Rhodes. Hopefully, Raven would be there when Turner was done, but if he wasn't, well, Turner would have to live without him.

He had most of his life, after all. It shouldn't be too hard.

Since Raven didn't know how to behave when it came to Turner or what to tell him, he decided that leaving would be for the best. He had no doubt Turner would have something to say about that, but at the moment, he didn't care. He didn't want to make things between him and Turner worse than they already were, so after making sure Turner was okay, he left the gym.

He didn't want to go home just yet, but he was at a loss. He shouldn't have agreed when Thomas had told him he'd make sure Raven wouldn't have too many shifts so he could take care of Turner. He should have known it wouldn't take the whole day and he'd have so much free time on his hands. He'd hoped he and Turner could spend some of that time together, getting to know each other, but he'd been spectacularly wrong, and now he didn't know what to do with himself.

Since he doubted that he'd see Turner again today and most of his friends were working, he decided to shift and go for a run. Maybe it would give him the opportunity to think things through.

Not that there was a lot to think about. For now, Turner seemed happy to continue training with Raven and not much more. Hopefully, that would continue, but Raven wouldn't swear on it. Turner had a precise objective in mind, and he was stubborn. Raven wouldn't have believed it, but he couldn't deny it, now that he knew Turner better.

He also couldn't deny he was attracted to Turner, but not

just that. Even though he was pissed at what Turner was doing, he also admired him. Turner had made a decision, and he was sticking by it, even though it was hard for him. It might not be the *right* decision, and he might be more pigheaded than stubborn most of the time, but still. It was something Raven could respect.

And he did. He just wished Turner would listen to him sometimes.

He dropped his clothes on a bench next to the gym entrance and shifted. Both he and his badger wanted to go back to Turner and make sure he was okay, but since Turner wouldn't take that well, Raven pushed the need away and turned to the forest instead. He ran between the trees, a stupid grin emerging on his face. He might not have any idea what to do with Turner, but he didn't have to find out now. Turner wasn't an idiot, and even though he wanted revenge, he wouldn't put his safety at risk. After all, who would kill Alpha Rhodes if Turner couldn't do it?

So, for now, Turner was as safe as possible, and Raven could focus on himself.

He ran between the trees, unable to remember the last time he'd done something like this. He wished he could do it more often, but it wasn't easy to find the opportunity when he was so busy. He supposed that was the case for everyone, though, and that he should stop using his job as an excuse. He wanted to make more time for himself, for his friends, and for things that weren't his job. If there was one thing that Turner had made Raven realize, it was that.

Turner didn't have anyone else because he hadn't let anyone come close to him. There were the other carriers, of course, but from what Raven had seen, Turner even kept them at a distance. It probably made sense in his mind.

After a while, Raven found himself in front of Jacob's house. He hadn't been here in a while, using the excuse that

Jacob and Chris had just gotten together and that they needed space to be with each other. It had been just that, though — an excuse. Now Raven was here, and he had every intention of spending time with his best friend if he was home.

He didn't want to shift back, so he climbed onto the windowsill and peered inside. He didn't know what to expect, but he wasn't surprised when Chris opened the kitchen door.

Chris smiled. "I hope you're not just a badger and that I'm not about to invite a wild animal into my home," he said.

Raven grinned. That was probably enough for Chris to realize he was a shifter and not a wild animal. Animals didn't tend to smile like idiots.

Chris gestured at Raven to walk in. Raven did, stopping to rub his face against Chris's leg. Chris laughed and scratched the top of Raven's head.

"Jacob's in the living room, if you're looking for him."

Raven grunted and headed that way. He found his best friend on the couch, reading something on his phone. Jacob looked up when he heard him, but Raven didn't give him time to speak. He rushed up Jacob's leg and settled into his lap, curling into a tight ball.

"Has something happened?" Jacob asked.

Raven couldn't give him details in this form, but he didn't think Jacob needed them. He relaxed under Raven when Raven shook his head.

"You just missed me, then," Jacob teased.

Raven twisted his head and glared at Jacob. Jacob laughed and scratched behind Raven's ear.

"Well, I have to go to work eventually, but you're welcome to stay here if you want. Just not in my lap, at least not once I need to get up."

Raven started to move off, but a gentle touch on his back made him stop.

"You don't have to go just yet. I have a little time before I have to go."

Raven sighed in happiness and relaxed into Jacob's lap.

A lot of people would find it weird for them to cuddle this way, but they'd been best friends for so many years that it felt natural. They were more like brothers than anything else, and being next to Jacob always made Raven feel better. He was still confused as hell when it came to Turner, but for the moment, he could forget about that and ignore both Turner and the rest of the world.

Jacob ran his fingers through Raven's fur, helping him relax even more. Raven was starting to fall asleep when Jacob gently tugged. "You shouldn't be doing this if it hurts you so much," Jacob whispered.

Raven didn't have to ask to know what his friend was talking about.

"I mean, I understand wanting to be with someone, and that's what you want from Turner, isn't it?".

Raven didn't answer. He could have shifted and talked to Jacob, but he didn't want to. It felt safer to stay this way.

Jacob sighed. "Remember Chris and me in the beginning? We were a mess, and we should never have let things go that far. In the end, everything worked out, but it doesn't always. I'm worried about you if you continue holding a torch for Turner. I'm not angry at him, and I understand why he's behaving the way he is, but he might not be the best choice for you, no matter how you feel about him. I can't tell you what to do, but I think you should remember that. Everyone has their own problems, and he's not any different. What *is* different is what he's been through in his short life. He's stronger than a lot of people I've met, but maybe that's part of the problem. He thinks he *needs* to be strong, and he doesn't allow anyone close, not even you. I'm not saying you should give up now or ever if that's not what you want, but think about it. I don't like seeing you so confused and in pain."

And Raven didn't like to feel this way, but could he give up Turner? He wasn't sure he could, no matter how much it hurt. It wasn't just that he wanted to be with Turner — and he did, even though he had no idea when it had happened. But Turner had wriggled his way under Raven's skin while Raven wasn't looking, and now Raven couldn't imagine life without him.

But maybe Jacob was right. Maybe Turner and Raven weren't good for each other, and Raven needed to accept at least the fact that they might not be. It was too soon for him to make any kind of decision, and there was no way to know how the future would turn out to be, but eventually, Raven would have to face the truth.

He wasn't sure he could let go. He had feelings for Turner, feelings he couldn't forget.

Feelings he couldn't ignore.

Every step Turner took was painful. He wasn't surprised, not after what he'd put his body through this morning, but he wished someone would have given him a ride home like yesterday. Instead, he had to hobble back to the Bishop house, and by the time he got there, he felt like he was about to start crying.

Unfortunately for him, that was when he crossed paths with Julian and Kaspar.

He tried turning around and leaving. He liked both men, and they were sweet and gentle. He wasn't up to talking with anyone, though, and he knew they'd be worried about him. He didn't want *anyone* to worry about him, but especially not Julian.

Julian was Kari's father, and he'd been through hell and back. He'd only recently found happiness with Kaspar, and even though it had been an accident, at least in Julian's case, both he and Kaspar were pregnant.

Turner couldn't imagine having two babies so close together, although he supposed it would be very much like having twins. The thought made him shudder in horror, and he was relieved the two had moved out of the Bishop house and into their own home. He didn't hate babies, but he didn't want to have to deal with them.

"What happened to you?" Julian asked, his voice conveying the horror he felt at the sight of Turner.

Because it wasn't just that Turner felt bad. He also *looked* bad.

The places where Raven had hit him yesterday had started bruising, which meant a lot of his skin was turning blue. The scratch on his cheek wasn't terrible, but it was still obvious, especially against the paleness of his skin. Between that and the way he was walking, he understood why Julian was horrified.

"Nothing. I promise," Turner said.

"That doesn't look like nothing," Kaspar said. His tone was lighter, thankfully.

"I've been training with Raven, and it's been going well. He's not pulling any punches, which is what I wanted." The last thing Turner wished for was for people to start thinking Raven was abusing him. "We cleared it with Thomas, so I promise everything is fine."

"I'm not your father, so I won't push, but we're taking you home right now," Julian said.

His voice said he wouldn't take no for an answer, and if Turner was honest, he didn't mind staying away from the Bishop house for a bit longer.

He didn't hate the other carriers who lived there. He liked them, some more than others, but all of them kind of felt like a family. They were just a lot to handle most of the time, and they reminded Turner of what he didn't want to be.

Coddled, taken care of, treated like he was fragile and unable to do things on his own.

He didn't berate any of them for taking advantage of what Thomas and the cete had offered them. They deserved everything they wanted in life, and if that was staying at the Bishop house forever, then that was what they should do.

But it wasn't for Turner. Turner wanted so much more, which was why he was working so hard to get it. He didn't know what would happen after all of this was over, and he didn't want to think about it. He just knew he couldn't be at the house at the moment.

So when Julian gently took his hand, he let the man take him away.

They walked between the trees, and it was oddly peaceful. Turner had lived in the forest his entire life, and while it hadn't been in this area, it was similar. He'd never felt so safe, though. He'd always known Alpha Rhodes wasn't a good person, but he'd been safe from him until the man found out he was a carrier. Once he had, Turner had known something would happen to him.

He'd been right.

"I can't believe Thomas agreed to this," Julian muttered.

"He didn't have a choice," Turner explained. "I told him I would find someone to train me even if he couldn't help me."

Julian chuckled. "Of course you did. You've never done things the easy way, have you?"

"Not really. But then, I don't think any carrier has ever done things the easy way. It's a curse."

"I don't think being a carrier is a curse."

"Neither do I."

Turner really didn't. Being a carrier was just what he was. It wasn't a good or a bad thing, not unless someone used it against him. No one would as long as he stayed with the cete, which he had every intention of doing. That was the only thing he was sure of when he thought about his future.

But knowing there was a life after this mission was soothing. He'd always have the cete as a home to come back to, no matter what happened. He couldn't see his future yet, but eventually, he would.

And he knew it would be here, with the cete.

"Here we are," Julian said.

They'd reached the house he now shared with Kaspar. The two of them didn't live alone, since Calum, another carrier, had moved in with them. Turner had been surprised, along with everyone else who knew him. Calum had always been a loner, even when the Bishop house had been full of carriers. They'd expected him to go back to the bats once he could, but instead, he'd begged Kaspar and Julian to take him with them. Turner didn't know why they'd said yes, and it was none of his business. Still, he wasn't sure he was looking forward to seeing Calum again.

The front door swung open, and Calum stood there, glaring. Turner started to get defensive until he realized that Calum wasn't glaring at him but rather at Julian and Kaspar.

He pointed a finger at them. "Where have the two of you been?" he demanded to know.

"We decided to take a walk," Julian answered. He didn't sound angry, but like he was used to this kind of reaction from Calum. He probably was.

"In this cold?" Calum asked. "What were you thinking? The two of you need to rest, not to go around running in the forest."

Turner was stunned, but it was obvious Calum cared about Julian and Kaspar. He was *fussing*.

"We're fine," Julian reassured him. "And we can't stay cooped up in here until the end of our pregnancies. You worry too much about us."

"Of course I worry about you," Calum grumbled. "How

can I not?"

"Should I remind you how much older I am than you?" Julian asked with a smile.

"There's no need for that. I know you're way, *way* older."

Julian laughed. "Exactly. We're fine. I promise." He hesitated. "But I'm not so sure about Turner. Would you mind getting coffee ready? I think he could use it."

"I'm okay," Turner tried to protest.

Julian shook his head. "You're not, but we don't have to talk about it if you don't feel comfortable." He hesitated. "We don't have to talk about anything you're not comfortable with. I just want you to know that both of us are here for you if you ever need us. I think that goes for a lot of people in the cete, but maybe you need someone to remind you of that."

"I promise I'm fine," Turner said.

"I think everyone here knows that's not the case, but all right. We can act as if we believe you—for now."

Turner snorted. "You really are a dad, aren't you?"

Julian grinned. "And I'm a dad to Kari. of all people. I'm sure you can imagine it wasn't easy, especially in the situation we were in." His smile faded. "I just don't want you to get hurt. I know your situation isn't easy. You were betrayed by one of the people who should have taken care of you."

Just like Julian. His alpha had raped him when he was little more than a teenager, and when Julian had realized he was pregnant with Kari, he'd decided to run. It had been the only way for him to keep his baby, and he and Kari had lived in the forest for decades, entirely on their own. It was only when Kari had met Calder and fallen in love with him that he'd been comfortable enough to bring his father into the cete's fold. Turner doubted Kari had imagined his father would find love and give him a sibling, but Kari was over the moon happy for his father, as was anyone who knew Julian. He deserved all of the happiness he could get, and he finally had it.

He was still very much a father, though, and it felt good to have someone who cared about Turner. Turner was surprised, but maybe he shouldn't be. He missed his parents, and sometimes, he wondered if they could have a relationship after Alpha Rhodes died. He hoped that was the case.

And if it wasn't, well, it was good that Julian had reminded Turner once again that he wasn't alone.

CHAPTER SIX

Turner was starting to get used to being sore and in pain all the time. He wouldn't have thought it possible, but he'd just finished another training session with Raven, and he didn't feel as bad as he had in the beginning. He wondered if it meant he was getting stronger, and he took a moment to think.

He and Raven had been training together for a few weeks now. They still weren't back to being friendly, and Turner wasn't sure how to make it happen. He just knew he didn't like the distance between them, but it was easier to ignore it than to try to do something about it. Raven had been taciturn, too, and maybe it was better this way.

But it didn't feel like it.

"That was good," Raven said. He grabbed the towel he'd left by the side of the mat and wiped the sweat off his face. "I'll see you tomorrow morning."

He started to walk away, but Turner had enough of this. "Wait," he called out.

Raven froze. "Yes?"

Turner wasn't sure what to say now that Raven had stopped to talk to him. He should have thought better about it, but now, it was too late.

"I'm sorry," he blurted.

Raven continued staring. "What are you sorry for?"

"For treating you like shit. You agreed to help me, and I've been bitching at you since the beginning. You don't deserve that. And I don't hate you. I was angry, which is the only reason I said that."

Raven crossed his arms over his chest. "I'm happy to hear that."

It wasn't the reaction Turner had expected or hoped for, but at least Raven was talking to him.

"I'm *really* sorry for everything. I shouldn't have sprayed you, and I shouldn't have yelled at you and told you I hated you."

Raven nodded. "You shouldn't have, no. Thank you for apologizing."

"I just want us to go back to what we had before. I don't know if it's possible, but I'd like to try."

Raven looked around. It was still early, but the gym was starting to fill up, which meant someone would probably overhear them. Turner didn't know what Raven wanted to tell him, but he obviously wanted some privacy, which was fine with him. He'd always disliked being the center of attention, and today wasn't any different.

"Let's step outside," Raven said.

Turner followed him into the cold. It felt good, since he was still sweating, but he knew Raven wouldn't keep him outside for too long because he wouldn't want him to get sick. Turner was getting used to people wanting to keep him safe and happy, and while it still made him uncomfortable, he didn't entirely mind. He was starting to realize people did that because they cared about him, and what more could he want?

"You're getting better," Raven said once they were outside.

Turner was disappointed. Was that the reason Raven had wanted to talk to him? To tell him he was getting better at fighting?

Turner swallowed. "Thank you. It's nice to hear."

Raven nodded. "You *are* getting better and learning, but it's not enough for what you're planning. I'd like to talk about those plans."

Turner sighed. In reality, it had been easier for him to focus on learning how to fight than on Alpha Rhodes. He was still planning on killing the man, but he had no definite plans. He couldn't project what would happen, but for now, it was good enough for him to continue doing what he'd been doing.

Clearly, it wasn't enough for Raven.

"Are you going to try to stop me if I talk to you about it?"

Raven hesitated. "It's the smart thing to do."

It was. Turner wasn't an idiot. He knew he didn't have a much of a chance to kill Alpha Rhodes, or if he succeeded, to come out of it alive. It was a risk he'd wrapped his mind around early on when he'd decided to do it, and he didn't feel it changed anything.

But Raven was right. No matter how hard Turner trained, it would take him years to be strong enough to defeat his old alpha. If he didn't want to wait so long, he'd need help.

Could Raven provide him with that help?

It wasn't something Turner wanted to ask of him. How could he? It would be too much to ask of anyone, but especially of someone Turner cared so much about. What would Raven say if Turner *did* ask, though?

To Turner's surprise, Raven reached for him and squeezed his shoulder. "Tell you what. Why don't we both go back inside and take a shower? I don't know about you, but I need one, and quickly, before I start repelling people with my stench. We can meet out here and take a walk, talk things out. I know you don't like to talk about it, but I think you should."

Turner's first instinct was to say no, but he forced himself to take time to think about it.

Raven wasn't offering to help him defeat Alpha Rhodes, but it didn't mean he wouldn't if Turner tried asking. It was a chance Turner couldn't give up without at least trying, which was why he nodded. "We can take a walk," he confirmed.

"Good. I'll see you out here in fifteen minutes?"

Turner nodded. He had no idea what was happening between them, but he knew that this was his chance. Even if he didn't manage to convince Raven to help him kill Alpha Rhodes, he wanted them to be close again. He'd missed Raven, and while he didn't understand why or when it had happened, he didn't care about those questions anymore. He just cared about Raven, and he wanted him back in his life as more than just a trainer.

He might not get what he wanted. Raven didn't like what Turner was planning, and he might make him choose between being friends and killing Alpha Rhodes. If he did, Turner wouldn't hesitate to choose his revenge—or at least, he thought so.

He wasn't sure about anything anymore, but he did know he couldn't allow Alpha Rhodes to continue hurting people. He supposed he'd have to see what happened after he and Raven talked. Until they did, he couldn't make plans, and trying would only make his head and heart hurt.

He followed Raven inside, since they were both going to the showers. Raven smiled at him once they were in the changing room and disappeared into one of the stalls. Turner watched him go, wondering what would be next for them.

Could they fix things? Was their friendship something Turner would be able to keep, or would he lose it?

He didn't know, but he supposed he was about to find out, at least in part.

Raven was happy to leave the gym. He'd seen a few people staring at him, even more at Turner. Even though the carriers had been with the cete for a while now, some people were still curious about them. A lot of people were interested in Turner especially. He was a gorgeous man, even though he didn't seem to care. Raven wouldn't have been surprised if a few badgers asked him out. He doubted Turner would say yes, because he was too focused on Alpha Rhodes and his vengeance, but eventually, he might want to date.

What would Raven do then?

Raven decided not to think about it. He didn't know what Turner would do in the future, and it wasn't his business anyway. He wanted to know what Turner's plans were, but only the ones that involved Turner killing a man.

"Thanks for this," Turner said as they walked between the trees.

It was cold, but both of them were dressed warmly. Turner had even wrapped a scarf around the bottom half of his face, which meant his voice came through a bit muffled.

"I know you like your privacy."

Turner pushed down the scarf and grinned. "I do, but it's so hard to get any when you live with so many people."

"The other carriers are still driving you nuts?"

"A little more every day, but I love them anyway. You know how it is."

"Not really. I'm an only child."

Turner nodded. "Well, most of the time, they're a lot to deal with. But I love them, and they love me. That's what matters, isn't it?"

"I suppose it is."

Turner was silent for a moment. "So, I wanted to apologize for the way I've been treating you," he said eventually.

Right. That was why they were out here right now. "You don't have to."

"I do. I've been an asshole, and it wasn't fair to you."

"I won't say you haven't been, but I understand."

"You shouldn't have to understand or treat me with kid gloves. I'm an adult man."

"You are," Raven confirmed as if there was a need to. "An adult man who was betrayed by one of the people who should have taken care of him. An adult man who's been through a lot."

Turner scowled. "That doesn't mean you should allow me to be a dick without consequences."

"I didn't. That's why we're here, isn't it? You wanted to talk to me and apologize, because my behavior toward you has changed."

Turner nodded. "It has, and I don't like it. In the beginning, I'd never have thought that I'd want to be friends with you, but I do. You aren't going easy on me, but being friendly while we train has made it easier."

"That was you being friendly?"

Raven was giving Turner a bit of a hard time, but he hoped Turner realized he was mostly teasing. They hadn't been friends, but he supposed things could have been worse. It had mostly been Turner trying to find a way to deal with his emotions and the fact that he'd told Raven what he was planning.

Turner glared. "I don't know how to be friendly. It's easier to keep people at arm's length than try to be friends with them."

Raven agreed, and he was guilty of doing it himself often enough. "I suppose we can be friends, and I can stop not talking to you."

Turner's shoulders slumped with what Raven thought was relief. "Thank you," he said.

"Don't thank me yet, because I'm not done. Now that that is out of the way, what are your plans?"

Turner groaned. "I was hoping you'd forget about them."

"Fat chance of that. How am I supposed to forget that you're planning on killing a man?"

"I don't suppose you could act as if you don't know anything?"

Raven was going to need all his patience with Turner. The problem was that he didn't know how much patience he was capable of. Usually he didn't have a lot, although things had been different with Turner. *Turner* was different.

"You can't be thinking of facing Rhodes without a plan," he said.

"Of course I have a plan. I might be doing something stupid, but I'm not an idiot."

"At least you realize that."

Turner glared, but Raven didn't care. If Turner insisted on doing this, Raven would tell him exactly how much of an idiot he was, and he'd point out the problems in whatever plan he was putting together.

"I don't have a plan yet," Turner said slowly, contradicting himself. "I know I'm not strong enough to beat Alpha Rhodes, but I'm getting better. You said that yourself."

"You are, but I hope you realize it won't be enough. I don't know what shape he's in or if he's ever been a fighter. But even if that's not the case, he has to know what people think of him and that a lot of them wouldn't hesitate to kill him. I can't believe no one has tried yet."

"Oh, I'm pretty sure someone has. They just haven't succeeded."

"And you think you will?"

"I hope I will. That's why I'm training."

"I really don't like this."

"I don't like it, either, but it's what I have to do. I can't live in the forest as long as he's still around. He's a danger to everyone, not just me or even just other carriers."

"I agree, but you just said yourself that you know you can't do it. Those two things don't go together."

"And what am I supposed to do? The council hasn't been doing anything. I don't blame them, and I understand their reasoning, but it doesn't help the situation."

Raven had to agree, and he'd been pretty vocal about it to his friends. Maybe it was time to tell Turner what he thought.

It might help Turner realize he wasn't as alone in this as he thought he was.

"I agree. I actually complained a few times about it, and I don't like that the council can't do anything about Rhodes. It doesn't mean *we* have to do something about it, though."

"And if we don't? Who's going to do it? Because Alpha Rhodes isn't an idiot. He's planning something. I'm sure of that. I might not know what it is, and I might never find out, but I can't just stay here and hope for the best. I did that once when I realized I was a carrier, and I'm never doing it again."

Raven could sense there was a story there, which wasn't surprising. "I do agree that something needs to be done about Rhodes, but it's not our job."

"Because we're not on the council? Because I'm not a guard but only a carrier?"

Raven scowled at him. "There's no *only being a carrier*. Stop acting as if I'm treating you like that's all you are. We both know I'm not."

"Fine, maybe you're not. I realize that by acting as if everyone is treating me like I'm weak, I'm pushing people away. I also realize I'm wrong. I guess it's a defense mechanism. I want to show people I'm strong before they think I'm not."

Raven was surprised Turner was admitting that, but he was also relieved. "I *know* you're strong. Carriers are some of the strongest people I've ever met. It doesn't mean I'm not worried about you, Turner. You want us to be friends? Well, this goes with that. Friends worry about each other, and they make sure their friends don't do something stupid."

Turner grinned. "You mean like trying to kill their old alpha?"

"Exactly. I don't want you to get hurt. No one here does, and Thomas will have my ass if something happens to you and he finds out I knew what you were planning. That's not why I don't want anything to happen to you, though."

"You don't want anything to happen to me because you care about me," Turner murmured.

Raven's heart raced. "I do. Everyone who knows you cares about you." Although, Raven doubted they all cared about Turner the way he did.

It was odd to hear those words coming from Raven. Turner had been so convinced Raven hated him that now it was a surprise to find out that wasn't the case.

"But why?" he asked. *That* was what he didn't understand. Why did Raven care about him?

Raven shrugged. "Why not? You're a good person. You're strong, stubborn, and you care about people. I see it every time you interact with your friends. I see how gentle and nice you are with Misha, how you listen to Hector ramble on for hours, how you eat Gallagher's cakes even though he burns almost all of them."

Turner snorted. "Everyone is nice with Misha. It's impossible not to be." As for the rest, well, they were his family. Of course he was nice to family.

"We both know that's not true."

Because someone hadn't been nice to Misha. Someone had raped him and forced him to carry a baby, and that was something Misha would never be able to forget.

Turner swallowed. "I still don't understand," he whispered.

"You don't see yourself clearly, but I'm not surprised. For so long, you were treated as nothing more than something to be sold. It's not right. It never was. It's not just because human beings shouldn't be sold, though. It's because of the way it makes you think of yourself."

Turner would be the first to admit he didn't have the best self-esteem. After all, he'd been told for a long time that the only thing he was good for was carrying children for an alpha. He knew that wasn't the case, but it was nice to have someone tell him. The cete had been so good to Turner and the other carriers that they couldn't deny they wanted them for more than just having children, but sometimes, it was hard to remember.

"So yes, I care about you, and I don't want anything to happen to you. But it's not just that."

Turner frowned. "What is it, then?"

"What do you think will happen if you kill Rhodes?"

"What do you mean?"

Raven gestured at the forest around them. "I know you want to kill him because of what he did to you and what he'll do to other people if we let him. But I'm talking about the forest in general. What happens when an alpha dies? Even more importantly, what happens when an alpha dies because someone killed him?"

Turner forced himself to think. He hadn't yet, and he probably should have.

In reality, beyond deciding he was going to kill Alpha Rhodes, he hadn't thought about much else. It would be a while before he could do it, and the consequences of that action still felt nebulous. It was a future he could barely imagine, and he couldn't allow it to distract him from his goal.

"Well, his son would take his place at the head of the skunks," he said slowly.

Raven nodded and gestured at him to continue. "Would he be a good alpha?"

"I don't know. I suppose he would be better than his father. He was never cruel, not to me anyway."

"Okay, so let's go with the assumption that Jasper would be a better alpha. What do you think the council would do if an alpha were killed?"

"In this case? Wouldn't they celebrate or something?"

Raven barked out a laugh. "Behind closed doors, probably. But the council was created to protect the shifters who live in this forest. They're there to make sure we don't kill each other and invade each other's territories."

"I know that."

"Okay, so what would they *have* to do if an alpha was killed?"

"I guess they'd have to investigate."

"Right. And what about the humans? We know those who live with us would have to send a report to their boss. They'd have to make sure the council investigates, and if they don't or don't find the person who killed the alpha, they'd probably have to step in and take over the investigation. Now, the council might be willing to close an eye if they find out you killed Alpha Rhodes, but what about the humans? Do you think they'd do that?"

Turner shook his head. "They couldn't." Even if they wanted to.

"Exactly. You see where I'm going with this? It's not only that you risk getting hurt. It's also that even if you manage to kill Rhodes, things won't just become perfect. There would be an investigation, and I don't want you to end up behind bars."

"I hadn't thought about it until now," Turner said. "But none of that will stop me. Please, Raven. I need you to understand. I don't want to be locked up and have to face a trial or whatever the humans will put me through if they find out I did this. I want to kill Alpha Rhodes because I want to be free, but I know I probably won't be. Even if I manage to survive killing him, I'll have to face everything you just described. I might not want to, but it won't stop me. I feel it's worth it to make sure Alpha Rhodes doesn't hurt anyone ever again."

Turner sucked in a breath. Now that he knew Raven cared about him, it was easier for him to understand the man. It made him want to get to know Raven better, but he couldn't let that stop him.

"I know you want to protect me," he continued. "And now that I understand it's because you care and not because you think I'm not capable of taking care of myself, it means a lot to me. But you *have* to stop protecting me. I need to do this, whatever the consequences will be."

Because Turner couldn't live his life if Alpha Rhodes was still alive. He'd never be able to relax, to allow himself to fall in love, maybe have a family one day. He'd be too scared that Alpha Rhodes would somehow manage to hurt the people he loved like he'd hurt him, and that wasn't something Turner could let happen.

He might lose everything if he continued on this path, but it was something he was ready to face and accept if it meant killing Alpha Rhodes.

Turner made sense, in a strange kind of way, and Raven wasn't happy about it. He'd wanted Turner to see what the problem with this plan was, and Turner did. The problem was that it didn't make him change his mind.

But Turner wasn't wrong. He was an adult, and after telling him and the other carriers again and again that they were strong and capable of making their life decisions, Raven couldn't exactly turn around and forbid him to do this. If Turner wanted to be stupid and kill Rhodes, it was a decision he was able to make.

Raven should step back like Jacob had suggested. This wouldn't end well for anyone, not for Turner, and not for Raven. Raven was going to have his heart broken, but it felt like nothing he could do would protect him from that. Even if he did stop talking to Turner, it wasn't like he'd stop caring about him. If anything, not knowing what was going on with him would make everything harder.

That meant that whatever Turner decided, Raven would be involved. He couldn't let Turner do any of this on his own, but he also couldn't let Turner kill Rhodes.

There might be a middle ground, though. "I want to help you," he said.

Turner stopped walking. "What do you mean?"

"With Rhodes. I want to help you."

Turner shook his head. "It's not your job."

"I don't care. Besides, it kind of is. I'm a protector. I'm a guard, which means that my job is quite literally to protect and guard people."

"But not from an alpha."

"You can turn this any way you want, but I'm not taking no for an answer. If you're doing this, so am I." And while Turner was stubborn, Raven would out-stubborn him.

"But I can't ask you to do that. You were the one just telling me how dangerous this was and how I stood to die or be imprisoned if I continued. Why would I want you to have the same fate?"

"You don't get it, do you? I'm not letting you do this on your own, whatever you say. Unless you decide not to do it anymore, I'm doing it, too."

Turner opened his mouth, but Raven was *not* listening to him complain. If Turner could make his own decision when it came to killing Rhodes, so could Raven. Besides, Raven still had hope that he would manage to change Turner's mind eventually. He wasn't quite sure how to do that yet, but for this, he'd find the patience.

Since he wanted Turner to stop complaining, Raven grabbed the back of his head and pulled him closer. Turner's eyes went wide, but he didn't push Raven away when Raven kissed him.

This time, Raven wasn't the one surprised. Turner was, but it didn't seem to be a problem, because he wrapped his arms around Raven's neck right away. He pulled himself closer, and Raven made a small triumphant sound at the back of his throat.

This was what he'd wanted since the beginning. He hadn't known it, and he still wasn't sure what he was supposed to do with Turner, but it didn't matter. Turner was in his arms, and they were kissing. *That* was what mattered.

And what a kiss it was. Turner was stubborn and opinionated, and that showed in the way he kissed, too. He knew what he wanted, and he didn't seem to have a problem taking it. He pushed his tongue into Raven's mouth, and Raven let him take over. Usually, he was more dominant in this kind of situation, but it didn't always have to be that way. He liked that Turner felt sure enough of himself to take what he wanted from him. After he'd been told time and time again that he was inferior to other shifters and only good for one thing, Raven wanted to give him this. He wanted to give Turner *everything*, and while he didn't know if he had it in him, he was going to try.

"Do you understand that I care about you now?" he whispered when they separated. Turner had never looked as good as he did now with his lips red and a hint of pink on his cheeks.

Turner nodded. He appeared to be a bit dazed, which made Raven feel incredibly smug.

"*This* is why I won't let you do this on your own," Raven continued. He didn't let go of Turner, cradling him against his chest. "I don't know what we're doing or if we can have anything. I suppose we'll find out eventually. We won't be able to if you insist on killing Rhodes on your own, though. Give me a chance, Turner. I'll show you how good we can be together."

"You sound very sure of yourself," Turner said.

"That's because I am. I know what I want, and in this case,

I want you."

"I still don't understand why."

"Does the why matter? Or does the fact that I want you matter more? I know you don't trust people, not even me, but I'm ready to do anything I can to change that. You just have to give me a chance."

"I don't want you to get hurt," Turner muttered.

"You mean like *I* don't want *you* to get hurt? I understand, and I think you do now, too. No one has to get hurt." Raven swallowed. This was what he'd been aiming for since the beginning, and he hoped he wasn't about to make a mess out of it. "Look, we don't have to decide to kill Rhodes right now. You said yourself that you're not ready for it, and I agree. How about we just start by watching him? It'll be the best way for us to learn when he's vulnerable and when we shouldn't even attempt to get to him. You know a lot about what happens in the surfeit, but things have probably changed, and we need to make sure of that before we decide to do anything. You don't kill someone without a minimum of research first."

Turner arched a brow. "Have you killed many people, then? Because it sure sounds like you have."

Raven glared at him. "You *know* I haven't, but it's not that different from any other kind of job. If you want to do something illegal, you need to know what you're working with first. That means research, which is the first thing we'll do. We'll also continue training. And once I feel you're ready and we have as much information as we can manage on Rhodes, we'll decide what the next step is."

And hopefully, by the time that happened, Turner would finally realize how stupid this was. Raven wasn't sure what he'd do if Turner didn't, but that was a hurdle he'd deal with when the time came.

Turner still didn't look convinced, but to Raven's relief, he nodded. "Fine. You can help me."

"Thank you," Raven said.

"Don't thank me yet. I bet you're going to want out of this in a week, tops."

Raven laughed. "Probably. Although now, I have an incentive to stay with you."

Turner arched a brow. "Do you?"

Raven kissed him again. He might not have any idea what they were doing or how Turner would react when Raven tried to stop him from killing Rhodes, but for now, none of that mattered. The only thing that did was the man in Raven's arms, and Raven had every intention of giving Turner one more reason not to kill Rhodes. Maybe if he showed Turner what he was standing to lose if he did something stupid, Turner would change his mind.

If he didn't, well, Raven would find another way. He wasn't letting Turner go, no matter what Turner believed.

CHAPTER SEVEN

"What is he doing?" Turner asked in a whisper.

Raven glared at him. "What part of silent didn't you understand?" he answered in the same tone.

"It's not like he can hear us," Turner said.

"He will if you continue talking."

Turner rolled his eyes but finally turned his attention back to the window they were watching.

The two of them were in skunk territory, spying on Rhodes. Raven had pointed out that Turner always mentioned his title when he talked about him, and that he wasn't Turner's alpha anymore. Turner hadn't realized he was doing it, but now that he did, he'd stopped. Sometimes, he still had the habit of adding the alpha title to the name, but he was doing his best to stop. Rhodes didn't deserve to be an alpha, and he didn't deserve for anyone to respect him as such.

Turner had been surprised that Raven had changed his mind after their talk in the forest. They'd spent the rest of their time together kissing, and while Turner had loved it, he'd also realized how much of a distraction it was. Now that he and Raven were together—or at least he thought they were—he wanted nothing more than to spend all of his time with him. Thankfully, the fact that they were training together helped, but Turner spent entirely too much time staring at Raven instead of doing what he was expected to do.

He supposed it didn't entirely matter. They were nowhere near ready to take care of Rhodes, which was why they were spying on him. He had time to be with Raven.

He'd guided Raven into skunk territory. He knew it well, having run around it since he was a child. Nothing had changed. However, he'd been relieved to see that the shed he'd been locked in was gone. He doubted Rhodes had been the one to get rid of it, so it had probably been Jasper, Rhodes's son. He and Turner had never been close, but Turner respected him just a tiny bit more because of that. He hoped Jasper would be a better alpha than his father, but if he wasn't, well, Turner supposed he'd have to take care of him, too.

Raven leaned closer, as if feeling that Turner's thoughts were spinning out of control. Both of them were sitting in a tree, the thick branch sturdy enough to hold both their weight. Turner had wondered if they should shift, but Raven hadn't wanted to. Turner supposed he didn't want to be vulnerable and naked in enemy territory, and he wasn't wrong. Rhodes would use anything he could to get rid of them if he saw them.

Turner had never wanted to come back. He'd known he would have to if he was planning on killing Rhodes, but he'd thought he'd have more time to wrap his mind around it.

Every time he heard something move, he jerked. He usually thought it was Rhodes, and when he didn't, he wondered if it was one of his parents. He hadn't seen them since Rhodes had taken him from his home, and knowing they were so close, yet so far, made him feel *things*. He wasn't quite sure what those things were, and he didn't want to analyze his emotions. Now wasn't the time or place.

Turner raised his binoculars again. Rhodes was behind his desk, doing something on the computer. Turner was curious and wondered if it was something that would hurt someone. Probably. He wanted to sneak inside and strangle Rhodes with his own hands right now, but he knew better than to suggest it. Raven would never agree.

"You've never told me about your parents," Raven whispered.

Turner blinked. "I thought you didn't want us to talk."

Raven narrowed his eyes. "He can't hear us. And if you want to talk about your parents, that's fine."

Did Turner want to talk about them? He wasn't sure. He'd just been thinking about them, though, and there would be no harm in telling Raven. "What do you want to know?"

"I'm not sure. I've never heard you talk about them, and I was curious."

Turner lowered the binoculars and settled his back against the trunk. "I guess they were normal parents. We were a normal family before Rhodes got to us."

"Did they try to keep you with them?"

"They did. They didn't want Rhodes to take me away, and they tried to fight it. They didn't think it was right."

"It *wasn't* right. Rhodes should never have been allowed to do that."

"He should never have been allowed to do a lot of things, but we both know how that went." Raven nodded, and Turner continued. "My mother wanted to run away with me. She told my father, but he was too scared. He didn't want to lose his wife along with his son, I suppose."

"So he didn't even try?"

"What would you have done? You don't know how it was to grow up here. You don't know what Rhodes did to us. You've always been with the cete, haven't you?"

Raven nodded, confirming it.

"Well, Rhodes has never been like Thomas," Turner explained. "From what I know, Rhodes's father was very much like him. They were in charge, and everyone had to go along with whatever they wanted. The entire surfeit was afraid of them, and there's no one to help them. Not even the council can. They can't get rid of Rhodes, and it would be too dangerous for anyone from inside the surfeit to try to do anything about it."

"There has to be a way for them to fight Rhodes without dying."

"Who told you that Rhodes kills people?"

Raven frowned. "No one. I assumed."

"You did. As far as I know, he hasn't killed anyone. No, what he does is worse. He takes us away from our families. He threatens us until we don't have a choice. If we don't do what he wants, our family will pay for it. Is that something you'd be willing to risk?"

Raven growled, probably in frustration. "None of this should have happened. He shouldn't have so much power."

"But he's an alpha. Now we have the council, and that's good, but it's not enough. The council doesn't have enough reach in the surfeit."

"That's why you want to kill him," Raven said.

"In part. I mean, in part, I just wanted to see his face before I kill him. I want him to know who it was and that even though he hurt me, I won."

Raven grinned. "So bloodthirsty."

"I'm not bloodthirsty. I just want him to pay, something that should have happened a long time ago. Since no one else can take care of it, I will."

"It sounds more like a good idea every day," Raven muttered.

Turner grinned at him. "Give it a few weeks, and you'll be clamoring to be the one to kill him."

"You're probably not wrong. The more I hear about him, the more I want to do exactly that."

Turner knew the feeling well. "And if I can't do it, I can't think of anyone who would be better than you. But yes, I want everyone here to be free to do what they want, and more importantly, not to have to give up a family member, not to be afraid their child will be hurt if they don't do what the alpha wants, or for carriers to be sold because of what they are."

"Do you think you'll talk to your parents again once this is over?"

"I don't know. I don't blame them for what happened, and I know they didn't have a choice, but it's still hard. I can't avoid thinking about the fact that they gave me up, even though they didn't want to."

"You'd need to forgive them, and you're not sure you can."

Turner nodded. "Exactly." But maybe, in time, he'd be able to forgive and forget. For the first time since he'd decided he would kill Rhodes, Turner thought he had a chance to make it out alive. With Raven, he had a better chance of that happening, which meant he might just have a future.

Would his parents be part of it? He didn't know, and he wouldn't find out anytime soon, but that didn't matter. The possibility that he could have them in his life again, that he could be free and do whatever he wanted with his life, was enough to get him to raise his binoculars again to look through the office window.

Raven hadn't expected Turner to answer his questions about his parents. Turner had been close-lipped about his life with the surfeit, and Raven had never pushed. It was none of his business, and he understood why it was so painful for Turner to talk about it.

He was glad they had. He felt like he'd gotten to know Turner a bit better, which was all he wanted. He had no idea what they were doing in their personal lives, but it was a good distraction for Turner so he wouldn't obsess over Rhodes, and Raven enjoyed the time they were spending together. It wasn't exactly what he wanted yet, but it was close, and he hoped that in time, Turner would want the same things he did.

He was angry with Turner's parents. He might never have lived under an alpha like Rhodes, and he understood fear, but he still couldn't wrap his mind around the fact that they hadn't even tried. What would Rhodes have done? Even if they'd been caught trying to get Turner out of their territory, it wasn't like Rhodes would have hurt him. He'd wanted to sell Turner, and he wouldn't be able to do that if he hurt him.

Raven could understand a lot, but he still would have some chosen words to tell Turner's parents if he ever met them. It wasn't his place, but it didn't matter. As long as Turner wanted him in his life, he'd protect him, even from his own parents. Turner might not *need* protection, but someone should still tell them they ought to treat their son better than they had until now.

Turner shook his head. "I don't know. I guess the only important thing is that I don't hate them and that I might be able to contact them in the future if I want to. Right now, I hate that I can't because of Rhodes and what he could do to me if I tried. I don't have a choice, you know? But once he's gone, I will, and I'll decide then. I don't know how I'll feel about them and what happened to me until all of this is over. I have too many conflicting emotions."

Raven nodded. He continued staring at Rhodes through the window, half tempted to go into the office right now and take care of the guy. He'd taken so much from a lot of people, including Turner. Raven wanted him to pay for that, and he was in a great position to do just that.

But he'd been the one who told Turner it would be stupid, and it would. He had to focus on that rather than on what Turner had been through, because otherwise he'd start making stupid decisions, and he couldn't afford for that to happen when he was in enemy territory.

Turner fell silent again, but it wasn't awkward. They

hadn't talked about what was going on between them, and Raven wasn't sure he wanted to. He doubted Turner would give him an answer, or rather, the answer he wanted, until this mess was over. Raven could only hope that Turner was falling in love with him the way he was falling in love with Turner and wait to see where things went. Pushing Turner would be the worst thing Raven could do. Besides, he still wasn't entirely sure how he felt about any of this. With everything Turner was going through, it would be too much to ask him to decide whether or not he wanted to be in a relationship, too.

But Raven wished he did.

"Something's happening," Turner murmured.

When Raven looked at him, he realized Turner wasn't staring at the office anymore. Instead, he'd turned his binoculars toward the front of the house. Raven did the same, wondering what Turner had seen.

Two cars were driving toward the house. They were too far away for Raven to be able to see who was driving them, but that wouldn't be a problem much longer because they were coming to visit the alpha. That was the only explanation Raven could think of.

Both he and Turner stayed silent until the cars parked in front of the house. Four men exited from both.

Raven leaned closer to Turner. "Do you recognize any of them?"

Turner took a moment to answer, which Raven liked. It meant he was truly thinking about the answer.

"No. I don't think any of them are skunk shifters. Besides, they drove in. Skunk shifters wouldn't have done that."

So Rhodes was visiting with shifters who didn't belong in his surfeit. There was no way this was a good thing.

Turner didn't like whatever was going on. Who were these guys, and what were they doing here?

Rhodes had never been one to work with others. He only did it when there was no other way for him to get what he wanted, and if that was the case here, Turner wanted to know what they were planning.

Nothing good, from the sight of it.

The front door of the house opened, and Rhodes stepped out. He was smiling, which also told Turner this couldn't be good.

He and Raven couldn't hear what was being said from that distance, but they didn't have to. Rhodes shook hands with all of the eight men visiting him. Then he gestured them inside the house. They went in, and he followed, closing the door behind himself.

"I think I got pictures of all of them," Raven said.

Turner blinked and looked at him. "Pictures?"

"Yes. When you said you didn't recognize them, I snapped as many pictures as I could." Turner finally lowered his binoculars and turned to look at Raven.

Turner had wondered what was in the backpack Raven had insisted they take along today, and now he knew. Raven had taken out a camera, and he was still holding it, pointed toward the office this time.

Turner would never have thought about that on his own, which was one more thing that made him realize he wouldn't have had a chance to take out Rhodes if Raven hadn't decided to help him. He hated admitting Raven had been right, but he had.

Turner raised his binoculars again and looked into the office. It was a large room, which was a good thing, because nine adult men were now stuffed inside of it.

"You know, I think I recognize at least one," Raven said, still snapping pictures.

"Which one?"

"The one with the mustache? I'm pretty sure he's a coyote shifter."

Turner frowned and looked at all the men until he found the one Raven was talking about. His mustache looked like it belonged in the eighties, but that wasn't what Turner was interested in. "Why would a coyote shifter be here? It doesn't make sense."

"It does if Rhodes is planning something and needs help. All his alpha buddies have been taken care of, so he can't count on them anymore. It looks like he has new allies, though."

At least they weren't alphas, but that was the only good thing about the situation. Them not being alphas didn't mean they couldn't hurt people, and Turner was afraid that was what was going to happen. "What do you think they're planning?"

"No way to know, unfortunately."

"Do you think we should move closer and listen to the conversation?"

Raven stopped snapping pictures just long enough to glare at Turner. "We are *not* moving from this tree. It's too dangerous."

"Whatever they're planning is just as dangerous."

"I agree, and we'll tell someone about this, but we're not going anywhere."

Turner's first instinct was to tell Raven to fuck off. He still thought Raven was trying to protect him every time Raven told him not to do something, and he was. Turner just had to remember Raven wasn't doing it because he thought he was weak, but rather because he cared.

Sometimes, that was hard to remember.

Turner looked back at the office. He desperately wanted to go in there, but instead, he stayed where he was. Raven was the only one between the two of them who knew what he was doing, and Turner had agreed to do this the way Raven wanted to. It would be stupid for him not to, and he *wasn't* stupid. He might have done stupid things before, and he would no doubt do them again, but not right now.

Because Turner knew what would happen if one of the men inside the office saw them. The thought terrified him, and he wasn't taking the chance, especially not with Raven being there. He didn't care if he got hurt, but Raven shouldn't. He *wouldn't*, not as long as Turner was there to protect him.

"You'll stay here?" Raven asked.

"I'm not going anywhere." And Turner meant that in more ways than one.

It didn't matter how badly Raven wanted to find out who those men were. It would have been stupid for him to stay, especially with Turner by his side. He snapped as many pictures as he dared, then he turned to Turner. "We have to go." He expected Turner to say no and insist they should continue spying, so he was both relieved and surprised when Turner nodded. He wanted to ask why Turner was being so amenable, but he knew better.

Raven scrambled down the tree, careful not to make too much noise. He looked toward the office as soon as his feet were on the ground, but no one was looking out the window. He couldn't see the office well from here, so he waited, one hand raised to tell Turner to do the same. Once again, Turner obeyed, staying where he was until Raven was sure no one was coming. Then Raven waved at him to come, and Turner did.

Turner stayed silent as they headed out of skunk territory. Raven didn't have to ask him where to go. Turner had shown him the way as they snuck in.

"What do you think he's planning?" Turner asked as soon as they were far enough that no one would hear them.

"I have no idea. You know him better than I do."

"It doesn't mean I know him well."

Somehow, Raven suspected that was a lie. Turner had to know the alpha. After all, he'd spent all of his life with the skunks. For whatever reason, though, he didn't want to talk about it, and Raven could understand that.

He was relieved when Turner stayed silent for the rest of the way to the car. Raven had parked it in the middle of some bushes so no one would notice it. The last thing he and Turner needed was for someone to find out they were here.

They climbed into the car, and Raven started the engine. The sooner they were out of here, the better. They could talk on their way back to the cete, but first, they needed to get out.

Raven only relaxed once skunk territory was far behind them and he was sure no one would think anything of seeing them where they were. Once he was sure they were safe, he peeked at Turner.

Turner was staring ahead, his back straight, his entire body tense, as if he expected his old alpha to come after him that minute. Rhodes just might, if he knew what they'd been up to. Thankfully, he hadn't noticed their presence.

Before they could talk about what had happened, Raven had to say something. "I want you to promise me you won't do something stupid," he said.

Turner jerked. "What do you mean?"

"You've been telling me you want to kill Rhodes for weeks. I know you haven't changed your mind and that you're humoring me, and I'm fine with that. But I need you to promise me again that you won't go out there and try to kill him."

Turner crossed his arms over his chest. "Don't you trust me?"

That wasn't an easy question to answer. Raven *wanted* to

trust Turner, but could he? He wasn't sure the answer was yes, not to this. He had no doubt that if Turner had an opportunity, he'd kill Rhodes without hesitation. That was what he wanted, after all.

"I do trust you," Raven said carefully. "And I didn't think you'd do anything, but I also understand emotions are running high right now. You saw Rhodes again for the first time in a while, and you're still angry."

"Wouldn't you be?"

"I never said it wasn't understandable. It is. Frankly, after what he did to you, I think it's a miracle that you haven't strangled him yet."

"And who's fault is that?" Turner muttered.

Raven found himself smiling. For all that he and Turner kept bickering, Raven liked him. He maybe more than liked him, but that wasn't something he was ready to deal with at the moment.

He did trust Turner not to go after Rhodes on his own, but it wouldn't hurt to distract him. Besides, Raven wanted to find out what Rhodes was up to, and he didn't think there was a way for him and Turner to do that without involving someone else. He just hoped he wouldn't regret this.

"I think we should talk to Jasper," he said.

"Jasper? You mean Jasper Rhodes?"

"Unless you know another Jasper?"

"I don't. Why would you want to talk to him? He's Rhodes's son."

"He is, and you were the one who told me you believe he'd be a better alpha than his father."

"That's because it would be impossible to be worse."

Raven didn't disagree with that. "So you don't trust him?"

Turner hesitated. "He's never done anything to hurt me," he said slowly. "He tried protecting me when his father stuck me in that shed. He used to sneak me food. Did you know that?"

"I didn't, no." There was a lot Raven didn't know about Turner's time in the shed.

"That doesn't mean he'll help us. He might not have been awful, but he's still his father's son."

"We could try talking to him and see what happens. We don't have to decide to tell him everything the first time we meet him."

When Raven looked at him, Turner looked skeptical. "And what will you tell him? *Hey, we'd like to talk about your father, but no worries, it's nothing bad?* He's not an idiot. He'll know we're up to something, and he'll want to find out what it is."

"We're going to have to take the chance, unfortunately."

"I don't like it."

"Neither do I, but he's the best person to ask if he knows what's going on. We need his help, and hopefully, we'll manage to convince him this is the right thing to do. Maybe we can mention the fact that he'll become the alpha after his father and that it'll happen sooner than he expects if he helps us."

"I don't think he cares much about becoming alpha. He was never like that."

"Hopefully, he'll want to help us because he thinks it's the right thing to do, then."

"I don't understand how you can have so much faith in him."

"I don't. I just know there's nothing we can do without help. We could go to Thomas, but somehow, I doubt you want that."

Raven wasn't surprised to see Turner glaring at him when he glanced his way.

"It's too dangerous," Turner said.

"So is planning to kill Rhodes. That hasn't stopped you."

Turner nodded. "This won't, either. It doesn't mean I have

to like it."

"I don't like it, either. But what choice do we have? Besides, asking for Jasper's help in this situation will help us understand what kind of person he is."

"Possibly. Or maybe he'll act the way we want to because he'll know what we're up to."

"Then we'll know what kind of guy he is, won't we?"

Turner huffed. "You can stop trying to convince me. I agreed, didn't I?"

He had, and Raven was still surprised. He wanted to ask Turner why he was agreeing so easily, but he knew that would be the best way to change Turner's mind and send him running the other way.

"So we agree? We'll talk to Jasper, try to understand what he thinks about his father's behavior, and possibly tell him that his father is up to something?"

"I still don't like this, but yes. We'll do that."

Raven prayed they wouldn't regret it, but he truly couldn't see another way out of this except by pulling Thomas into it. Turner would never agree to that, though. He wanted them to do this on their own, but Thomas would insist on doing it the right way if he found out. He wouldn't be wrong, but Raven didn't want to betray Turner, not unless it was necessary.

He hoped he wouldn't have to. Turner would never speak to him again if he went behind his back, and while Raven was ready to do that if it meant saving Turner's life, they weren't quite at that point yet.

Hopefully, they wouldn't get there for a while longer.

CHAPTER EIGHT

Turner stared at Jasper.

He and Raven had been following the other man, trying to understand what kind of person he was and to find the perfect moment to talk to him about his father. No matter how long they watched him, though, Turner still wasn't sure what to think of him.

Jasper seemed like a nice enough guy. He didn't spend a lot of time with his father, or in skunk territory, for that matter. It was almost as if he'd washed his hands of the surfeit, which Turner didn't appreciate. It wasn't his home anymore, but Jasper would be the alpha eventually. He should pay more attention to the skunks.

Of course, it was impossible to know what Jasper's father would let him do. Maybe there was a good reason for Jasper not to spend more time with the skunks. Maybe he wasn't authorized to. Turner wouldn't be surprised if that was true. He'd known Rhodes all his life, and the man disliked not being in full control, both of himself and of the people around him. He was probably afraid that if Jasper gave the skunks too much attention, they'd want him to be alpha instead of his father. That wasn't how it worked, but Turner wouldn't be surprised if Rhodes felt that way.

Besides, it *could* work that way. If enough skunk shifters wanted Jasper to take his father's place as their alpha, they could make it happen. It wouldn't be easy, and they'd have to stop being terrified of Rhodes long enough to act, but it wasn't impossible.

Somehow, Turner still didn't think that would be enough for them to do something about it.

For now, Jasper was in Northwood, away from his father and the skunks. Turner had expected him to have a lot of friends, and he'd been surprised to see that wasn't the case. If anything, Jasper seemed to be a loner. He'd been spending most of his time on his own, sitting in coffee shops and spending hours in bookstores. Turner wasn't sure what it meant, but it seemed to be enough for Raven, who'd decided they ought to talk to Jasper as soon as possible. That didn't sound like the best idea.

"I don't think we should talk to him in this coffee shop," Turner tried.

Raven snorted. "If it was up to you, we'd never talk to him."

"There's a good reason for that."

Raven's expression softened. "I have no doubt you have a good reason to feel that way. You were the one who told me you didn't think Jasper is dangerous, though."

"No, I told you I wasn't sure, not that I didn't think he was a danger. And I wasn't lying. I honestly don't know what to think of him."

"We'll find out soon."

"What if he pitches a fit in the coffee shop? Do you really want to get everyone's attention that way?"

"He won't do anything. He's not an idiot."

Turner wasn't a hundred percent sure of that yet, but he'd told Raven how he felt about it. Raven had listened to him and dismissed his fears. What else was he supposed to do?

"I hope we won't regret it," he muttered as he and Raven walked into the coffee shop.

"We won't," Raven promised.

Turner prayed he was right.

There were a lot of shifters in the coffee shop. In the

beginning, it had been a shock for Turner to see so many different shifters living together, but he'd gotten used to it while living with the cete. It wasn't the same, because the cete was still its own group, a sort of family, while the shifters in Northwood didn't belong to any group, but it was similar enough that Turner didn't feel too uncomfortable.

Jasper was sitting at a small table at the back of the room, reading a book. He didn't notice them until they were right next to him. When they were, he looked up, a half-smile on his face that froze as soon as he recognized them.

"Turner?"

Turner gave him a grimace that might have passed for a smile. "Hi, Jasper," he said.

Jasper gaped. "What are you doing here?" His gaze moved to Raven. "Are you on a date?"

Turner snorted. "Not exactly." He and Raven had never been on a date. They hadn't had time, and while Turner couldn't help but wonder what it would be like, he had other things to focus on.

"We're here to talk to you," Raven declared as he pulled one of the chairs away from the table and sat in it.

Jasper blinked. "You want to talk to me?"

"That's what I just said."

Jasper looked around. "What do you want to talk to me about?"

Turner sat, too. He didn't want to be the only one on his feet, and since he wasn't sure whether or not Jasper would pitch a fit when he found out why they were here, he didn't want to get too much attention.

"Your father," Raven said.

Jasper jerked as if Raven had hit him. "I don't want to talk about him," he said.

"That's a pity, because we're going to talk about him anyway," Raven said. He looked uncompromising, his expression telling Jasper to shut up and listen.

Turner hoped he would.

"We'd like to know what your father is up to," Raven said.

"I don't know." Jasper's answer was instant.

"How can you not? He's your father, and you're the next alpha."

"It doesn't mean my father tells me anything about his business. You found me here, which means you've been following me. *That* means you know I don't go back to skunk territory often enough to know what's going on there."

Turner leaned forward. They didn't have time to waste, dammit. "You know what your father did to me. You were there for most of it. You helped me. Do you really want this to continue happening?"

Jasper's cheeks flushed, and he looked away. "I'm sorry for what he did. He should never have been allowed to, but what am I supposed to do? I'm nothing to him. You know that, Turner. You know he doesn't care what I think about him."

"We're not asking you to try to change his mind. I just want to find out what's happening." Turner hesitated. Telling Jasper about this might be a bad idea, but he didn't see another way out of it. "You're right. We've been following you, as well as him. I've always known he wouldn't stop, even with the new laws in place. That's how Raven and I found out he was planning something. He's been talking to shifters who don't belong to the surfeit."

"So? He talks to a lot of people."

"He does. He also hurts a lot of people, Jasper. Please. You know what he did to me, what he's going to do to other carriers if he finds any. Will you let him to continue doing this? You might be the only one who can stop him."

"I can't do anything," Jasper protested. "You can't expect me to go against him."

"That's not what we're asking," Raven interfered. "We just

want to know what he's doing."

Jasper snorted. "Just? You don't know what you're asking me to do."

"We do. You forget that Turner knows exactly the kind of person your father is. He knows what that man is capable of, which is why we're asking this of you. You can continue saying no and hide your head in the sand, or you can at least listen to what we have to say and keep an open mind."

"He's my father," Jasper murmured.

Turner could understand why Jasper wouldn't want to go against his father, but Jasper needed to look the truth in the face. His father was a monster, and he could either fight against him or be on his side.

Jasper looked like he was about to bolt, which Raven hoped he wouldn't do. Raven couldn't exactly run after him, not if he wanted to keep this meeting a secret—which he did. The worst thing that could happen right now would be for someone to find out they were talking to Jasper.

To his surprise, Turner reached for Jasper's hand on the table. "I know who he is," he murmured. "I realize it can't be easy for you to go through this. But you have to see that what your father has been doing is wrong. He's been hurting people who haven't done anything to deserve it. He's been hurting people like *me*, who just want a life and to be left alone. Will you really permit that to continue?"

Jasper looked away. Raven expected him to tell Turner to fuck off, get to his feet, and leave, so he was surprised when Jasper stayed where he was.

Instead of leaving, Jasper looked at Turner. "I'm sorry for what he did to you. He shouldn't have."

Turner nodded. "You're right. He shouldn't have, and you should have stepped in when he did."

Jasper winced. "He'd have locked me in that shed with you. I did what I could."

"Maybe you did. Maybe at the time, it was enough. Are you doing what you can now, though?"

Jasper sucked in a breath. Raven hadn't known what to expect from this meeting, but he was glad he'd brought Turner along. Turner seemed to understand what to say to Jasper more than Raven could. After all, they shared an experience Raven had never gone through.

Jasper sighed. "Fine. What do you want from me?" he asked.

Turner leaned back. "Find out everything you can about your father and the men he's been talking to. We need to know who they are and what they're planning."

"You realize that finding that out won't be easy. My father doesn't trust me, so he won't talk to me, even if I ask. Hell, I *can't* ask, not unless I want him to realize something is going on."

That wasn't anything Raven hadn't expected. "You don't have to talk to him," he intervened. "You'll have to sneak around and try to find out what he's up to. Do you think you can do that?"

Jasper sighed. "I don't have a choice, do I?"

"You always have a choice."

Jasper scowled. "Why doesn't it feel that way, then?"

Raven felt kind of sorry for the guy, but not much. If he'd been in Jasper's place, he'd have been doing everything he could to get his father out of the way. He understood not everyone was like him, though, which was why he was giving Jasper a chance. Jasper was walking on thin ice, though.

"Fine. I'll do what I can to find out who these men are. Happy?" Jasper asked.

"We won't be happy until we know for sure what your father is up to, but it's a start."

Jasper scowled. "It might be a start for you, but it could be the end of my life."

Raven suspected he was being a bit overly dramatic, but maybe not. He knew his father better than anyone else, so he'd know what Rhodes was ready to do to protect himself and his plans.

But that wasn't Raven's problem. Jasper could either decide to do the right thing or to continue doing the wrong one. Raven and Turner couldn't make the decision for him. No one could.

Jasper got to his feet. "I'll see what I can do. I'll call you if I find anything."

"Will you?" Raven asked.

"I'm doing what you've asked of me. Isn't that enough?"

"We won't know until we find out what your father has been up to."

"And I just told you I'd help as much as I can. That's all I can promise."

Hopefully, it would be enough. But as Raven watched Jasper almost run out of the coffee shop, he had his doubts. It didn't *feel* like enough, but Turner wasn't going to like his next suggestion. "I think we should talk to Thomas."

Turner jerked. "What?"

"You heard me. This is getting out of control, Turner. We know Rhodes is up to something, and we can't keep that to ourselves. It wouldn't be right."

"But we don't know for sure that he's up to something," Turner protested. He leaned closer. "Yes, we saw him with those people, but we have no way to know what they're doing. Maybe it's nothing, and we'll look like idiots if we go to Thomas."

"I don't mind looking like an idiot if it means having help and doing the right thing."

"But maybe I do. Maybe I don't want people to think I'm

crying wolf. Please, Raven. I understand that you want Thomas to be involved and that he should be, but we should wait until we're sure Rhodes is planning something. I promise that as soon as we are, we'll go to Thomas together."

Raven wasn't an idiot. He could tell Turner was lying, but he still wanted to go along with what Turner wanted. Maybe that did make him an idiot, after all. What did it say about him that he couldn't resist Turner's puppy eyes?

He was worried and really wanted to talk to Thomas, but Turner wasn't wrong. It wouldn't hurt to wait for a bit longer, just long enough for them to be sure of what Rhodes was doing. They'd just asked Jasper to help, after all. They should give him time to actually do something.

He sighed. "All right." He didn't want Thomas to be pulled into something there would be no coming back from.

Not yet, anyway.

Thomas was the badger alpha, and he had other things to focus on. Hopefully, Rhodes wasn't actually up to something dangerous. If he was, well, Raven supposed they were about to find out.

He was done thinking about Rhodes, though. He sat up in his chair and smiled at Turner. "I won't talk to Thomas yet. I think we should go on a date, though."

Turner blinked. "I'm sorry?"

"You heard me. I want you to go on a date with me."

"What do you mean?"

"I mean that we're in Northwood, and that since we haven't gone on a date yet, we should do it now. How often do you come to Northwood? What do you want to see now that we're here?"

It was a bit nuts, but Raven wanted time away from Rhodes and whatever he was doing. It would be good for Turner and for him, too. He was entirely selfish suggesting it, though. He wanted Turner to be his and his alone for one afternoon.

Surely that wasn't too much to ask?

Or maybe it was. At the moment, Raven found he didn't care. He wanted to forget about Rhodes and all their problems for just a few hours. And while Turner might resist, Raven was pretty sure he could convince him.

He offered Turner his hand, and Turner took it without hesitation. "Come on a date with me," Raven murmured. "I know we have things to do, but it's a waiting game right now. We have to wait for Jasper to get back to us with news about his father. Until he does, there's nothing we can do."

"We could spy on Rhodes again."

"We could, but what good would that do? Come on, Turner. Go on a date with me."

How was Turner supposed to say no? He'd never expected those words to come out of Raven's mouth, but now that they had, he *couldn't* say no.

And he didn't want to.

"I've never been on a date," he confessed.

Instead of scaring Raven off, that made him smile. "That's fine. Unless you don't want to?"

"I do. I'm just not sure what you expect from me."

"I don't expect anything, Turner. I know who you are and what you went through. I know none of this is easy for you." He smiled deprecatingly. "Nothing with you is ever easy, and I didn't expect it to be when I started this with you."

Instead of making Turner angry, Raven's words made him grin. "And what did you start with me?"

"I'm not sure, but then, that's what this date is for, isn't it? We can find out how we work together when we're not spying on people and making plans to kill them."

Turner laughed. "There's no one else I'd rather have my first date with."

Raven got to his feet and offered Turner his hand. "Good. Come on, then."

They left the coffee shop, still holding hands. It felt odd, but not bad, and Turner was more than happy to go along with it. He swung their hands a little, peeking at them every so often until Raven caught him doing it. Raven didn't berate him for it, though. Instead, he smiled at him.

"What did you have in mind?" Raven asked.

"I'm not the one who decided we should go on a date. Shouldn't *you* be the one to decide what we do?"

"We're on this date together, which means we should decide together. I'm sure you've thought about going on a date. What did you imagine when you did?"

Truthfully, Turner had never allowed himself to imagine he'd have a boyfriend. It would have hurt too much when he'd known what his future was supposed to be like.

His parents had managed to hide that he was a carrier for several years. They'd found out when he was a teenager, and he mostly stayed home, only leaving the house when absolutely necessary. He'd gone to the tiny surfeit school, but he hadn't let himself have friends, and he certainly never allowed himself to tell anyone what he was.

Then they hadn't been able to continue hiding it, and Rhodes had found out. Turner was lucky he'd been twenty-five by then, but on the other hand, it meant he'd spent years hiding out in his home. He hadn't had friends or a boyfriend. He'd only had his parents, which was why it had hurt so much when they'd given him up, even though he'd always known it would eventually happen.

"I have no idea what a date is about," he eventually said. "But I trust you."

Raven stared at Turner for a moment before nodding. "Thank you. I know you don't trust easily, and it means a lot that you trust me."

They continued walking, and Turner was happy to go along with whatever Raven wanted. In the back of his mind, he couldn't help but wonder if they should allow themselves to be distracted. They needed to focus on Rhodes and what he was up to, and going on a date wouldn't help with that.

But Raven was right. They'd been spying on Rhodes for a few weeks now. And apart from that day when those guys had visited him, he hadn't done anything strange. Until Jasper called them and told them what his father was up to, there wasn't anything else they could do. They couldn't go back to spy on Rhodes, because eventually he'd see them. It would be best for them to stay away until they had something more concrete, and Turner supposed that going on a date wasn't a bad idea.

Eventually, they stopped walking. Turner had been so distracted that he had no idea where they were, and he looked around, curious.

They were in front of a restaurant. Turner had never eaten in one, and he was curious but also a bit worried. He didn't have a lot of money, but that wasn't a problem. He could pay for half of the meal if that was what Raven wanted. He just wasn't sure whether or not it was expected of him.

"Is this okay?" Raven asked.

"You mean if I want to eat here?"

"Yes. We don't have to if you don't want to."

"Well, we have to eat, don't we? We might as well do it here."

Raven didn't seem offended that Turner wasn't more enthusiastic. He just smiled and pulled Turner toward the door, and Turner followed.

He'd seen enough movies to know what to expect on a date, but he wished he'd already been through one. He didn't want to ruin things with Raven, and he was pretty sure that would be easy for him to.

He let Raven pull out his chair and help him settle at the table. Then Raven sat next to him instead of in front of him, and Turner was lost. Were they supposed to look each other in the eyes as they ate? They wouldn't be able to do that if Raven was on the same side of the table.

Raven took Turner's hand and squeezed. "I just wanted to be close enough to touch you," he murmured.

Turner swallowed. So that was why he'd settled next to him rather than in front of him. "I like touching you," he murmured.

Raven's smile widened. "I like touching you, too. So, what do you want to eat?"

Turner grabbed the menu in front of him. He hadn't even realized they were in an Italian restaurant, although he wasn't surprised. Wasn't that where everyone went on their first date? "I'll have the lasagna," he declared.

Raven nodded. "It's pretty good here. It's a good choice."

"You've already been here?"

"With friends, yes."

Turner had to keep in mind that, unlike him, Raven had a life before they met. "That's nice," he murmured.

Raven nodded and started talking about who he'd come with and what they'd eaten, but Turner tuned him out.

What was he doing? Should he be here? He wanted to be, and he wanted to date Raven and to be able to say Raven was his boyfriend, but he could get hurt too easily, and he wasn't ready for that.

Raven leaned closer after giving the order to their waitress. "Relax," he whispered. "Nothing is going to happen that you don't want."

"I know you wouldn't do that."

Raven shook his head. "That's not what I meant. You're right that I wouldn't do anything you don't want to, but I was thinking of you."

Turner frowned. "What do you mean, then?"

"That I'm sure you have a list of specific things you believe should happen and not happen on a date, and that you're worrying yourself sick thinking you have to do them. Would it help you to think about this as a dinner between friends?"

But that wasn't what Turner wanted. "We're not just friends."

"We can be whatever you want. We don't have to label this if you're not comfortable with it. I'll do whatever you want, Turner, as long as you tell me."

"I want to get to know you." Even though they'd been spending a lot of time together, Turner still didn't know a lot about Raven, and the same went for Raven. They'd been focused on Rhodes and spying on him, on making plans, but maybe it was time to change that. Maybe, for once, Turner could forget about Rhodes and his plans and focus on Raven. It might not be the smartest thing to do, but it was the only thing he wanted to do right now, and he was going to do what he wanted.

Raven relaxed, although not entirely. He was used to being the one who wasn't comfortable on dates and didn't know what to do, but this time, things were different. *Turner* was different, and Raven wanted him to be comfortable. He wanted the date to be great, but he wasn't quite sure how to make that happen.

The easiest way was to go along with whatever Turner wanted, which was what Raven decided to do. Things were a bit awkward initially since neither of them seemed to know what to say, but they both relaxed once their food was in front of them. Turner ate with gusto, making small sounds of pleasure that made Raven want to grab him, drag him into his lap, and kiss him.

Instead, he turned his attention to his spaghetti. Turner had said he wanted to get to know him, but Raven wasn't sure where to start. He might have decided to take Turner on a date, and he might have a bit more experience than Turner when it came to this, but not much. He couldn't even remember the last time he'd been on a date. He didn't usually bother, but then he didn't usually care about people as much as he cared about Turner.

"What will you do once this is over?" he eventually asked because one of them had to start.

"You mean if I survive?"

Raven glared at Turner. "That's not funny."

"I didn't say it to be funny. I just don't want to fool myself by thinking I'm definitely going to make it out alive."

"You will. I'll make sure of it. You have to remember that you're not alone anymore. Your main goal might be to kill Rhodes, but mine is to keep you alive."

And Raven would do everything he could to make that happen. If it meant he had to do something Turner wasn't okay with and that Turner never spoke to him again, well, he'd do it anyway. Turner's life was more important than them being together.

Turner leaned back in his chair and looked upward for a moment. "Honestly, I've never thought about it. I know that if I ask Thomas to help me find a job, he will, but I have no idea what to do. I don't even know if I'm good at anything. Besides, even though the laws have changed, how many people in the forest will hire a carrier?"

"Thomas will find you something."

"I know. And I'll talk to him once this is over. I suppose it's good that I have time to think about what I might want to do. Have you always known you wanted to protect the cete?"

"Not really. I was just more comfortable staying within the cete than trying to find a job here in Northwood, and there's a limited number of things you can do if you want to work inside your shifter group. I'm happy with what I do, though."

Turner nodded. "It's obvious when you do it. I mean, you go hard on me when you train me, but you're good at what you do, and you never push too hard. I can see you teaching once you're done protecting the cete."

Raven had never thought about that. "I don't think I have the patience to teach anyone."

"You had it to teach me."

"But you're special."

Turner's eyes widened just a bit. "Am I?"

"To me, you are. I don't think I'd be able to do this with anyone else. I'd want to slam their head against the wall. Besides, I'm too busy to start teaching people."

"No one said you had to do it right now. Maybe it's something you should think about for the future. Eventually, you might want to settle down with someone and have a family."

"Is that what you want? A family?"

"I'm honestly not sure. I know I don't want children until I feel the forest is safe, but will that ever happen? Even if we kill Rhodes, there'll always be someone who wants more power, who believes other people are inferior, or whatever. I'm starting to realize that there isn't a right moment to have children."

"I agree." But now that they were talking about kids, he couldn't help but imagining Turner carrying his child.

Raven had never thought about having kids. He didn't have anyone special in his life to have those kids with, so he hadn't needed to. He was with Turner now, though. Could he have kids with him?

He could imagine it, at least, which he supposed was a step toward that. There was no way to know if he and Turner would be together in the long run, but then, the same went for anyone Raven ever had a relationship with.

The conversation moved to a lighter topic, for which Raven was relieved. They continued talking through the meal. When they left in the car, Raven drove straight to the Bishop house, since it was getting late. He didn't want the evening to end, but he hoped they could do this again.

He parked in front of the house. It was late, and all the lights were off inside. That didn't mean Turner wouldn't be safe. There was no safer place in the entire forest than the Bishop house.

"I had fun," he said, turning toward Turner.

Turner nodded and unhooked his seatbelt, and Raven followed his lead. "So did I. Thank you for pushing for this."

"I didn't have to push a lot."

"Because I wanted to spend time with you. I'm glad I did."

Raven hesitated. Should he walk Turner to the front door? Or would Turner get offended? Raven never wanted Turner to think he believed he was weak, but he wanted to take care of him the way he would for any other person he'd date. The problem was that he didn't know if Turner would allow it.

Before he could make a decision, Turner swung toward him. Raven had just the time to reach up and grab Turner's hips before Turner was in his lap, facing him.

Raven swallowed. "Turner?" he asked.

Turner shook his head and kissed Raven. Raven had no idea what was going on, but he was more than happy to go along with it. He'd let Turner set the pace and decide whatever they were about to do. Raven was up for anything, as long as Turner was happy with it.

He kissed Turner back, wrapping his arms around him and pulling him closer. Turner wiggled for a moment, moaning when his hardening cock brushed against Raven's. There was no hiding either of them was hard, but Raven didn't *want* to hide it. He wanted Turner to know exactly what he was doing to him.

And Turner did know. He reached between them and swiftly undid Raven's jeans. Raven never wore underwear, finding them uncomfortable, which meant that his cock sprang out of his jeans, brushing against Turner's hand.

Turner jerked away, but that only lasted a moment. Then he moved forward again, wrapping his fingers around Raven's cock.

Since Raven didn't want to be the only one to feel pleasure, he went to work on Turner's jeans. Turner seemed eager as he thrust his hips forward, which made Raven smile. He wanted everything with Turner, and this was a good start.

He grabbed Turner's cock, pulling on it and grinning when that made Turner groan. Turner stopped kissing Raven, tilting his head back, his face toward the roof of the car. It was so dark Raven could barely see anything, but he didn't have to in order to know that Turner was enjoying himself.

Turner's hips jerked forward, and their cocks brushed together. Turner moaned again, and Raven couldn't resist anymore. He was going to come if Turner continued jacking him off, but he wouldn't be coming alone.

He let go of Turner's cock and wrapped his hand around both their dicks. Turner whimpered and tried to move, but Raven didn't allow him to. Instead, he jerked his hand up and down, jacking both of them off. Turner moved his hips in the same rhythm and buried his face against Raven's neck. Raven kissed what he could reach of Turner's skin. It wasn't enough, but they had time. They could do this again and again until they knew each other's bodies like their own. It would take time, and Raven couldn't wait.

Turner shuddered in Raven's arms just as Raven felt his cock jerk. He came, slicking Raven's fist with his seed. It pushed Raven that much closer to orgasm, but what really did the trick was when Turner gently bit on Raven's neck.

Raven shouted and came. Turner held him through it, and

once they were both done coming, they slumped in each other's arms. Raven took a deep breath, inhaling their mixed scents.

He couldn't wait to do it again.

But then Turner moved, breaking the spell. "I should go inside."

"Of course."

Turner quickly pushed himself back into his jeans and closed them. "Do you think anyone saw us?"

Raven looked at the house. "I doubt it. There's no one else there, and all the lights are off."

Turner nodded. "Good."

Raven told himself it wasn't because Turner didn't want anyone to know about them. He just had no idea what he was doing, and this was his first sexual experience. Raven was humbled that Turner had wanted to be with him.

He cupped one of Turner's cheeks, thankfully doing so with his clean hand. That got Turner's attention, and Raven gently kissed him. "I'll see you tomorrow?"

Turner nodded. "You will. We have training, right?"

They did, but that wasn't why Raven wanted to see Turner.

Turner got out of the car and closed the door, then scurried toward the house. Raven watched him go, waiting until the door was closed behind him to put himself to rights and turn on his car.

He had no clue what was happening between them, but he cared about Turner, and he thought Turner cared about him. For now, knowing that was more than enough.

CHAPTER NINE

Turner had been restless, which he suspected was the only reason Raven had agreed to come spy on Rhodes again. They didn't really need to, or at least, Turner didn't think so. Since that meeting, Rhodes hadn't done anything strange as far as Turner and Raven had seen, but Turner had been going nuts not having much to do.

He and Raven had been training, like always. They'd also been dating, although they hadn't gone back to Northwood. They'd seen each other in badger territory, and that was more than enough for Turner. He'd never had a boyfriend, and sometimes having one was still strange. He was glad he could get used to the feeling in a place where he felt safe.

But there wasn't much for them to do, and Turner knew he'd been driving Raven bananas. He'd been surprised when Raven had suggested going back to skunk territory and checking on what Rhodes was doing, but he couldn't say he minded. It was very much the opposite.

Sitting in a tree spying on Rhodes was starting to become his and Raven's thing. It was no doubt strange, but it was very *them,* and Turner was glad. He wanted to have something that he only did with Raven beyond sex. He had friends now, but he only had one boyfriend, and he liked that their relationship felt special.

Of course, it would probably be best if their special thing wasn't spying on a monster.

Raven's arms tightened around Turner. "Everything okay?" he asked in a whisper.

Turner nodded. They were sitting in the same tree where they'd been the last time they spied on Rhodes, but their positions were different. Instead of just sitting next to one another on the branch in a precarious balance, Raven had straddled it right by the trunk and pressed his back against the tree. Then he'd dropped his arms around Turner and pulled him against his chest. Turner's back was toasty warm, but, more importantly, he was in Raven's arms. That was all he cared about, although he realized he shouldn't. There was more to them than the cuddling, and they had other things to focus on, but he couldn't find it in himself to be miffed about their position.

Turner had no idea what to expect from a relationship or from Raven as a boyfriend. He'd been surprised to see how affectionate Raven was, but in a good way. He'd known Raven cared, but having Raven show him just how much he did felt good. It had been a long time since Turner had felt so loved, and he wanted more of it. He felt he would always want more of Raven, which was a good thing, since Raven always seemed to want to give him more.

A vibration made him look back to smirk at Raven. "Is it your phone, or are you just glad to be next to me?" he asked.

Raven barked out a laugh. "If that were my dick, I'd be worried."

Turner wasn't used to anyone talking that way, but it was freeing, and he found himself grinning back. Raven wiggled a bit until he managed to get his phone out of his jeans pocket. He peered at the screen, and Turner held his breath. It was probably nothing, but there was no way to be sure, and he was always a bit nervous these days. A phone call could be nothing or everything.

"It's Jasper," Raven said. "He texted me."

Turner straightened so quickly that he almost toppled both of them off the branch. Only Raven's hand clamping on his hip kept him where he was.

"Easy there," Raven murmured.

Turner nodded, not even caring that he'd almost fallen. "What's he saying?"

"Just that he has news."

Turner scowled. "That's it? He couldn't give you more details?"

"That's not a bad thing. He doesn't want to say anything on the phone, and I agree. It could be dangerous."

Turner had to remember that he wasn't alone in this, and that Raven, and probably Jasper, knew better than he did what to do in this situation. Still, it wasn't easy to have to wait, and he glared at Raven. "When are we going?"

"Right now, if you want."

"Of course I want to go now. Did you think I was going to wait? Rhodes isn't doing anything anyway."

"I'm aware." He patted Turner's hip. "Come on. Let's go."

Turner was more than happy to obey. He scrambled off the branch, careful not to fall and get Rhodes's attention. He peered at the house once he was on his feet, but nothing was happening.

"Did Jasper say where he was?" he asked when Raven joined him.

"No. He didn't even say he wanted to see us, just that he has news. Should we head to Northwood?"

"How should I know?" Turner bit his lower lip. "How about we go to his house?"

"Here in skunk territory?"

"He might not be home, but he also might be, and if he is, we'll be able to see him right away."

Raven nodded. "Lead the way."

Turner did, careful of their surroundings and who was around. They didn't see anyone as they headed to Jasper's house, though, for which Turner was grateful. He always half expected to see his parents when he and Raven were around. He didn't think they'd do anything if they did see him, but he couldn't be sure, and he hated that.

Would Turner's father go to Rhodes if he found Turner in skunk territory? Would Turner's mother be able to stop his father if that was the case?

Turner didn't have answers to those questions, and he didn't want to think about it anyway.

He led the way to Jasper's little house. Thank God it wasn't close to his father's, which meant Rhodes wouldn't see them. As far as Turner remembered, Rhodes barely visited his son. It should be safe enough for Turner and Raven to be there, and he hoped he wouldn't be proved wrong.

"This isn't what I expected," Raven said once they stood behind the house.

"What *did* you expect?"

"I don't know. I mean, he's the alpha's son, so I guess something bigger."

"Jasper isn't like that."

Raven looked at Turner for a moment before nodding. "I'm getting that impression, yes. I don't think you're wrong when you say he wouldn't be a bad alpha."

Turner stared at the house for a moment. He didn't want to go to the front because it would increase the danger of being seen, but there was no way to know if Jasper would hear them at the back door.

So instead, he decided to sneak in.

There was an open window there, and he pushed it completely open. Raven seemed amused, but he didn't say anything and followed Turner's lead. Turner was grateful. He knew he was a bit ridiculous, but it didn't matter. Raven was there, and he'd always have his back. That was the one thing Turner was sure of.

Turner looked around once they were inside. They were in

Jasper's kitchen, and while he couldn't see Jasper, he could hear him. Music drifted from the front of the house, so he headed there, Raven following him.

They found Jasper in the living room, dusting. That wasn't the only thing he was doing, and Turner almost started laughing when he found Jasper shaking his ass to the music. It wasn't what he'd expected, but he supposed he didn't really know Jasper. They'd never been friends or even friendly.

He waited until the song was over to clear his throat. Jasper screeched and twirled around, holding the cloth he was using to dust to his chest. When he saw Turner, he glared.

"What are you doing in here?" Jasper asked.

"You said you had news for us."

"And that gave you the right to come into my house?"

Turner shrugged. "We were around." He moved deeper into the room and flopped onto the couch. "Well? What did you find out?"

Jasper glared, but he sat down in an armchair. He eyed Raven as if he expected Turner's boyfriend to do something, but Raven just stared back.

"I know why those people were visiting him," he eventually said.

Turner straightened. "And?"

Jasper grimaced. "You're right. They *are* planning something, and it's not good."

For once, Turner wished he *hadn't* been right. "Tell us."

"They want to take out the council. That's why they've been meeting. I don't know how they're planning to do it yet, but they'll find a way. You know my father. He won't hesitate to do anything to get what he wants, and in this case, he wants to get rid of the council."

And as Jasper said, Rhodes would do anything he could to succeed.

What the fuck were they supposed to do?

133

Raven wasn't surprised. He'd imagined Rhodes was up to something like that. It was the only thing that made sense, considering he was working with shifters who didn't belong to his surfeit. "I didn't think your father could work with different species," he said.

Jasper shrugged. "I'm just as surprised as you. He doesn't usually work well with others, not even other skunks. But yes, the fact that he's working with other shifters is odd."

"And not in a good way." Not as far as Raven was concerned. It made Rhodes and the shifters he was working with even more dangerous, which wasn't something Raven wished for.

Turner's plan to kill Rhodes was looking better with every day that passed.

"How did you find out?" Turner asked.

"How do you think? I spied on him when he had a meeting the other day."

"And you didn't call us to tell us about this meeting?"

Turner sounded angry, but that wouldn't help in this situation. Raven went to stand behind the couch Turner was sitting on and squeezed the back of Turner's neck. It helped Turner settle, and Raven nodded to himself.

He noticed Jasper looking at them, but he didn't care who saw them or who realized they were together. He wasn't ashamed of being with Turner. If anything, he was incredibly proud.

"What would you have done?" Jasper answered. "You'd have come and spied on him, but you'd have been outside. It was better for me to spy from inside."

Turner looked like he wanted to argue, but in the end, he settled down and nodded at Jasper to continue.

Jasper did. "I've been hanging around his house after you

asked me to spy on him. When I saw two cars in front of it, I knew something was happening, and I snuck inside the house. I grew up there, so I know all the nooks and crannies and the spaces to hide. I heard everything they told each other."

"So you know what there've been planning?"

"They didn't go into details, and I think it's because they don't fully trust each other."

Turner snorted. "They're right not to."

"I agree, but do you want to hear what I heard?" He waited for Turner to nod. "They don't really have a plan yet. I think they're still working out how to work together, which is good."

"Is it?"

"You tell me—if they can't work together, they won't be able to do anything to the council."

"What's to say they can't work together?"

Jasper shrugged. "Nothing. It could be worse, though. They might already have a plan in place, and that's not something you want."

Jasper didn't have a whole lot to say after that. Raven wasn't surprised he hadn't been able to find out more, but he wished he had.

Raven and Turner snuck out of skunk territory and headed back to the car, which was parked in the same place Raven had left it the last time they'd been here. Turner had been silent, but that wouldn't last forever. He always did that. When he found new information, he took his time thinking about it and considering all the angles. It was something that made Raven proud. Turner wasn't acting on instinct like he'd been in the beginning, when he was so angry and ready to retaliate against Rhodes. He was thinking things through, and that could only be good.

"I think it's time to tell Thomas," Raven said once they

were in the car.

That got Turner's attention. "Not yet," he protested.

Raven turned the engine on. He'd already known this would be a fight, which was why he hadn't brought it up again until now. "Why not? We know Rhodes is planning something for sure."

"We don't know what it is, though," Turner pointed out.

Raven snorted. "Neither does Rhodes, for that matter. I don't think we have a reason to continue waiting."

"And I think we do. What do you think Rhodes is going to do if he finds out we know?"

"Not much, considering he doesn't have anything. You heard Jasper. It's a miracle his father is managing to work with those other shifters. I don't think we need to be afraid of what they're up to yet."

Turner crossed his arms over his chest. "Then why tell Thomas?"

He had Raven there. "Because he needs to know. This isn't only about you anymore, Turner. It's about the entire forest and how dangerous Rhodes is. And you know he is, even though he hasn't done anything yet. Don't hide your head in the sand."

"I want to be the one to take care of him," Turner declared.

Raven had always known this would be a problem, so he wasn't surprised. "I understand that. I really do. But maybe it's not the best thing."

"You changed your mind?"

Turner sounded angry but also disappointed, which Raven didn't like. He never wanted to disappoint Turner. "I didn't, but you have to see that might not be possible. It's not because you're weak, if that's what you think I believe."

Turner's shoulders slumped. "I know you don't think I'm weak," he said.

Raven was relieved. "I don't think you fully understand

what you're getting yourself into. I don't think any of us know, which is why I don't want you to do this. We don't know what Rhodes is planning exactly, and I don't like that. I also don't like the thought of you fighting him on your own."

"I wouldn't be on my own. I'd be with you."

"I know." And he would. Raven wasn't letting Turner do this on his own, but if he could avoid it at all, he wasn't letting Turner do it, period. "We need to rethink this," he said, praying Turner would understand. "Please, Turner. I don't want to lose you."

But when Raven peeked at Turner, he thought he already had.

Turner looked pissed, and Raven had no doubt that as soon as he stopped the car, Turner would be out of it and running. He didn't know what to do to stop him from doing just that, or even if there was anything he *could* do. He wanted to protect Turner, even from himself, but he didn't think he could. Turner's expression was enough to tell him that, but no matter how hard he thought as he drove, he couldn't come up with anything that would keep Turner with him and safe.

Turner was angry. He couldn't believe Raven had lied to him, or maybe he could. What had he expected? Of course Raven had lied. He'd wanted Turner to do what he asked, and the best way to make that happen was to lie.

And now Raven was going back on his promise, and Turner didn't know how to take it. He was angry, disappointed, and he wanted to kill Raven. What hurt the most, though, was to realize he might have trusted the wrong person. He didn't want to believe it, but the facts were in front of him.

Raven was trying to get Turner to change his mind. He'd sworn he would let Turner do this, yet he wasn't going to.

Turner was sure of that. What did that mean for him? What did it mean for him and Raven as a couple?

Turner had no answer, even though he desperately needed one.

"You promised," he said. He could hear the hurt in his voice, so he had no doubt Raven could, too.

Raven kept his focus on the road, but Turner knew he had all his attention.

"You promised, too," Raven said." Remember? When I agreed to help you, I told you that we'd have to talk to Thomas eventually. You told me we would, but once again, you're saying no."

Turner looked out the window. Raven was right, even though Turner didn't want to admit it. He had promised they'd go to Thomas, yet, he was going back on his word. Even worse, he'd always known he would because he'd never had any intention of going to Thomas. He'd known what Thomas would do, which was to pull Turner away from his mission.

"Something is going to happen, and soon," Raven said. "I know Jasper made it sound like his father and the others don't have a plan yet, but I don't believe that. Maybe Rhodes hasn't told all of his allies about it, or maybe there's something else going on. I don't know, but Rhodes isn't going to stay quiet for long, and we have to do something. We can't ignore what's going on."

"We're not ignoring it," Turner said through gritted teeth.

"Aren't we? Because to me, it looks like it's *exactly* what we're doing. I know you wanted to face Rhodes on your own, and I understand. We can't do this alone, though. Rhodes is working with other people. We have pictures of some of them, but I doubt they're the only ones he's working with. What if you go in there and find he's not alone? What if we kill him, but the plan goes ahead because he wasn't the only one working on it? Are you willing to take that risk?"

Turner hated when Raven made sense. He didn't want him to. He wanted to stay angry, but it was hard when Raven was so calm.

It didn't matter. Turner was stubborn, as was his anger. "I think we can deal with all of them on our own."

Raven snorted. "You were never stupid, Turner. Don't start acting like you are now. There's no way we can take on nine men alone, no matter how hard we train. Nine against two is never going to happen."

"Maybe we just have to take out Rhodes. He's the boss here. Once he's gone, the others will stop what they're doing."

"You can't be sure of that."

"And you can't be sure we won't be able to take him." They were almost in badger territory, and Turner was getting desperate. "Please, Raven. You promised you'd let me do this."

"And you promised we'd talk to Thomas if things became too dangerous."

"I have to be the one to kill Rhodes."

Raven stayed silent, which Turner suspected didn't bode well. He kept his mouth shut as Raven drove them into badger territory. To Turner's surprise, he didn't go to the Bishop house, but rather to his own place. Turner didn't know what to think of it or what it meant.

Raven parked the car but didn't leave it. Instead, they both sat in silence for a moment.

"All right," Raven eventually said.

Turner blinked. "All right?"

Raven nodded. "I'll wait to talk to Thomas." Turner opened his mouth to tell him how thankful he was, but Raven wasn't done. "I have one condition," he added.

Turner eyed him, wondering what that condition would be. "What is it?"

"We won't do this alone. I understand why you want to do

it on your own, but we both know it's stupid. You'll end up killed, or worse, and I don't want that to happen to you. No one here wants it."

Turner didn't want to be hurt, either, but he didn't want to make that promise. He didn't want anyone to try to stop him from doing what was right, which, as far as he was concerned, was killing Rhodes. Still, he knew Raven wouldn't let go until he promised. He felt slightly guilty doing it when he didn't mean it, but he knew it was the only way to get Raven to agree. "Fine. We'll talk to Thomas when the time comes."

Raven grunted. "I think the time has already come, but all right. I'll give you a little longer. This can't go on forever. You know that."

Turner did. He was going to have to do something, and soon. That something would hurt Raven, and there was nothing Turner could do about it.

He had to choose between Raven and killing Rhodes. He knew which he wanted to choose, but also which one he *should*.

Unfortunately, it wasn't Raven.

Raven was going to lose Turner. He could tell, even though Turner was smiling at him as they finally climbed out of the car.

He didn't want to hurt or betray Turner, but he wasn't an idiot. Turner had been lying through his teeth, which really wasn't surprising. Turner had no intention of ever going to Thomas if he could avoid it, no matter what Raven said and what Turner promised.

Raven swallowed. He didn't know what to make of this or if there was anything he could do about it. He doubted that was the case. He'd have to deal with it when the time came, which, unfortunately, would be way too soon.

He needed to tell Thomas. It was the only thing that made sense, but the thought made Raven's stomach churn. Thomas might already know what Turner had been planning, but he wasn't aware of what Raven had agreed to, of the fact that they'd been spying on Rhodes, or that they knew that Rhodes was planning something. He was going to be angry, which Raven understood. He was ready to endure whatever punishment Thomas thought was right, but he didn't want Turner to have to pay, too.

He didn't want to lose Turner, but it was too late.

What was the alternative? Not say anything and wait for Turner to get himself killed? Maybe Raven didn't have to talk to Thomas, but who could he talk to?

He tried to think as he and Turner walked into his house. Maybe he could talk to Jacob or even Alex. They'd both be pissed, but they might understand.

No. Raven had to go to Thomas and tell him everything. He'd lose Turner, but it was the only thing he could do. He had to keep Turner safe, even from himself.

It hurt so much more than Raven had expected. He knew it was because he and Turner had become close and were together, and he didn't want to lose that.

It was better to lose that than to lose Turner, though. That was what would happen if Raven didn't step in, and he couldn't let it.

So tonight, he was going to betray Turner.

Raven swallowed and turned to his boyfriend. "Are you staying?" he asked.

Turner shrugged. "I doubt you want me to."

"Of course I want you to stay. Why wouldn't I?"

"We've been fighting."

"This wasn't a fight. It was a disagreement."

"Really?"

"Really. Are you staying, then?" Raven wanted him to, but

he wouldn't beg. Besides, it would be better if Turner went home so that Raven could go to Thomas right away.

Turner kissed Raven's cheek. "I think I'll go home, actually. Misha thought he had some contractions the other day, and I want to be there for him."

Raven found himself smiling. "Go be with your friend, then."

"I will. Call me later?"

"Of course." Once Raven would be done betraying him.

Turner kissed Raven on the lips, then turned around and left. Raven watched him go, knowing it was probably one of the last times he'd do so. As soon as Turner found out what Raven had done, he'd refuse to talk to him ever again, and Raven would have lost him.

That wasn't enough to stop him from leaving his house.

He felt like shit the entire time it took him to walk to Thomas's house. He knew that was where he'd find his alpha, and he was right. When he walked in after knocking, Thomas's wife told him Thomas was in his office, and Raven headed straight there. Thankfully, Thomas was alone. As soon as he saw Raven's expression, he knew something had happened. Thomas was one of the few people Raven trusted with his life, or, in this case, Turner's.

"What's going on?" Thomas asked.

Raven told him everything. He explained that he and Turner had been spying on Rhodes, that he had pictures of some of the men visiting with Rhodes. He told him they'd contacted Jasper and that Jasper had agreed to spy on his father for them. He explained what Jasper had found and what he thought was going on.

He left out that he and Turner had become boyfriends, because it wouldn't last long now anyway. Thomas was a good alpha, though, and he could tell there was something else. He didn't push, but once Raven was done talking, he leaned back in his chair and stared at him.

"You're hurting," he said simply.

Raven wasn't going to cry, but it sure felt like he was. Instead, he nodded. "Turner is going to hate me when he finds out I talked to you."

"The two of you are friends."

"We're together. Well, we were."

Thomas's expression shifted. "I see. I can't say I expected it, but it does make sense. Maybe you won't lose him."

Raven snorted. "We both know I will. There's no way Turner will ever want to talk to me again once he finds out I talked to you."

"I'm sorry, Raven."

"I am, too, but this is the only thing I can do. He's going to get himself killed if I don't intervene, and I can't let that happen."

"Don't tell him about this meeting," Thomas said.

"I can't lie to him." Not any more than he already had.

"It won't be forever. I just want to look into what Rhodes is doing better, and if Turner finds out you talked to me, he might go off halfcocked and get himself killed. I know you don't want to lie to him, and I don't like it, either. I just don't think we have a choice."

Thomas was right, and knowing that made it even more painful. Not only was Raven betraying Turner, but he wasn't even going to be honest about it. Turner *really* was going to hate him by the time this was over.

"I won't tell him," Raven agreed.

Thomas gave him a small smile. "Thank you. If I'd known how much this was going to hurt you, I would never have asked it of you."

"But if you hadn't, I wouldn't have been happy with Turner for a bit. What is it that author wrote? That it's better to have loved and lost than never to have loved at all?"

"Something like that. It still doesn't feel right."

"But life isn't right. It's painful and raw, and I knew what I stood to lose when I decided to do this. It's not your fault, Thomas. I won't hold any of this against you, because it wouldn't be fair."

"None of this is fair," Thomas murmured.

Raven agreed, but what was he supposed to do? He'd already lost Turner, even though Turner didn't know it yet. At least Thomas was giving him a chance to spend a little more time with Turner before Raven lost him forever.

CHAPTER TEN

Something was wrong with Raven. Turner didn't know what, but he was sure there was something. Raven had been acting strange over the past few days since they'd bickered about going to Thomas. In the beginning, Turner had thought Raven was angry at him for not wanting to go. He'd have understood if that was the case, but Raven had sworn it wasn't, and Turner didn't think he was lying. There was something else, but he didn't know what.

He also didn't know how to find out.

He didn't like fighting with Raven. Raven had become an important part of Turner's life, and he wanted their easy relationship back. He realized it was his fault that they'd lost it to begin with, but he didn't know what to do about it. He doubted that talking to Raven would help. They'd been talking and talking since Raven had agreed to help Turner, but something was still happening with Raven.

Turner was almost afraid to ask, but it made it hard to focus on what was important, which was Rhodes. *That* was what he needed to think about, not Raven and their relationship.

Maybe that was the problem. Maybe Raven had realized he didn't want to be with Turner and didn't know how to tell him. Turner wouldn't be surprised if that was the case, and while he wanted to find out for sure, he had other things to focus on.

He'd promised Raven they'd go to Thomas soon, but he'd been lying. That made him feel awful, and maybe that was why he felt Raven was hiding something. Maybe Raven wasn't, and Turner was just projecting.

But they were close to getting to Rhodes, and Turner pushed his thoughts back to that.

He and Raven had been training together and gathering more information on Rhodes and the people he was meeting with. They had a list of names now, and they knew the group was going after the council. Turner believed that meant they'd be taking it over if they could. They wanted complete control over the forest, and that was the best and easiest way to get it.

The thought of Rhodes in control of the entire forest made Turner's stomach churn. It was easy to imagine what Rhodes and his friends would do if they ever were in power, and he didn't want that to happen. The problem was that he didn't know if there was a way out of it. They might know that Rhodes was planning something, but they didn't know what exactly or how it would happen. Not knowing was terrifying, but Turner felt a bit better knowing Raven was with him. He'd keep Turner safe, and Turner would do everything he could to keep Raven safe, too.

"We just need to find out what their plan is," he said.

Raven grunted. They'd just finished training and were walking home together. Raven had been silent the entire time, even more than he usually was.

"How can we find out?" Turner continued talking. "Maybe we should sneak inside Rhodes's office. Do you think he wrote something down?"

"He'd be an idiot if he had," Raven said.

His tone was curt and not at all how he usually talked to Turner.

But Turner was afraid to confront him. If Raven didn't want him anymore, he didn't want to find out. He wanted to focus on the fact that they were together for now and imagine himself with Raven for years to come. He doubted that would happen, but he wasn't ready to face it.

"We could hack his computer," he offered.

"You know how to do that?" Raven asked with a drawl.

Turner glared at him. "I don't. At least I'm putting out ideas. I can't say the same about you."

Raven glared right back. "What do you want me to do? I'm already helping you as much as I can and going against everything I believe in doing so. We could have help from someone who actually knows what they're doing, but you don't want that."

"We can do it."

Raven shook his head. "I'm not as convinced of that as you."

Turner's stomach twisted. "What's going on?" he asked, instantly regretting the words.

Raven looked at him for a moment before shaking his head. "Nothing."

That was *definitely* a lie, but Turner was afraid to ask, so he didn't. Instead, he said, "We should call Jasper again. He might be able to help. He found out that his father was planning on attacking the council, after all."

"You'll put him in danger if you continue using him. His father will find out about him eventually, and you know better than a lot of people what Rhodes is capable of."

Turner winced at the reminder. He hadn't needed it. "What then? We can't just sit back and do nothing."

"We're not doing nothing. We wouldn't even know Rhodes is planning something if we hadn't been spying on him. That ought to count for something, doesn't it?"

"But it's not enough." Turner was tempted to do something stupid, like going to Rhodes and killing him before Raven could talk him out of it again. The only reason he didn't was that he wasn't ready. He'd probably end up dead if he tried, and while he was ready to die if it meant taking care of Rhodes, he wanted to avoid it if at all possible. Raven had given him something to live for, and he didn't want to lose it.

But for now, they were stuck. Turner had no idea what to do when it came to Rhodes, just like he had no idea what to do when it came to Raven. He was lost, and he didn't like that feeling.

He didn't like any of this, but, unfortunately, he couldn't see a way out of it.

Raven was an asshole. He'd betrayed Turner, and he hadn't told him. Turner was going to be so pissed when he found out. Raven wouldn't be surprised if he hit him. He wouldn't try to stop him, either. He deserved for Turner to hit him, then to never talk to him again.

He loathed the way Turner was looking at him right now, like he wasn't quite sure what to say or do to make Raven feel better. Nothing he *could* do or say would make that happen. Raven needed to tell him what he'd done, but he was afraid. He didn't want to lose Turner, which would no doubt happen once he was honest.

So instead, he was lying. He was trying to act as if nothing had happened, even though he was pretty sure Turner had realized something had. He hadn't said anything about it, but then, he seldom did. Raven thought he was too afraid to shake things up because of how little experience he had.

God, he really was an asshole.

But if telling Thomas meant that Turner was safe, Raven would do it again. He didn't like betraying Turner, which was why he was keeping his distance. Being close to Turner meant talking to him, and he was afraid he'd tell him everything.

"This is getting too dangerous," Raven said. "There are different shifter groups involved, and we don't know in what capacity. As far as we know, one of the new alphas is involved, too, and we can't afford to go against more than one group."

"Why would one of the new alphas be involved? They all work with the council, and they agreed to the laws."

"It doesn't mean they're okay with them. We don't know what's happening, Turner. You can't take risks."

Turner his expression turned mulish. "But *you* can?"

"I never said anything about that."

"No, but you're a guard. You know what you're doing, and I don't."

Raven didn't want to fight. He didn't know how much longer he had with Turner, but it wouldn't be long. What was happening was his own fault, but he couldn't explain that to Turner. "Yes, I know what I'm doing better than you," he said. "But I still wouldn't go against Rhodes and his friends on my own. It would be foolish."

Turner's shoulders slumped. "I know. I'm not going to do something stupid, even though I'm tempted. I made you a promise, didn't I?"

"You did, and you weren't happy about it."

"Of course I wasn't. I'm still not. When you started training me, you promised I'd be able to go after Rhodes. But you haven't allowed me to."

"Because we now know things we didn't before. We had no idea he was working with so many other shifters. Now, we do, and it's dangerous. You have to know that I don't want to put you in danger."

Turner shook his head. "It's no use talking about this. We've been talking about it for weeks, and we still fight over it. Nothing's going to change that."

Raven agreed, yet he was tempted to continue fighting. At least it meant Turner was talking to him.

He looked ahead. "As long as you admit you and I aren't equipped to deal with this on our own and that revenge isn't the right solution, we're fine."

Turner opened his mouth to answer, but, thankfully, they'd reached the Bishop house. Two of the carriers were on the porch, and they started waving when they saw Raven and Turner. It was almost as if they hadn't seen Turner in weeks rather than a few hours, and Turner rolled his eyes at them. Still, he seemed to enjoy the attention, which told Raven everything he needed to know.

"They're ridiculous," Turner muttered as they reached the porch steps.

Gallagher grinned. "But you love us anyway."

"Sometimes, I wonder why."

"Because we're lovable," Hector intervened.

"I wouldn't be too sure about that," Turner said. "What are two of you doing out here? Is something wrong? Is it Misha?"

Gallagher shook his head. "The baby's still inside. Do you think Misha's going to explode soon? Because he sure looks like he will."

"People don't explode," Hector said.

"Are you sure? Because he's not looking good."

"What do you mean?" Turner asked. "Has something happened?"

"Everyone is fine," Hector soothed. "Especially Misha. Well, he's miffed because he's not allowed to move from the couch, but he's fine. Gallagher's just getting bored."

Turner rolled his eyes. "That's because you're all stuck in this house. You need to leave for a bit and explore the world outside of it."

Gallagher's gaze moved from Turner to Raven. "You mean like you have?"

Turner huffed. "Yes."

"So we should find ourselves a boyfriend?"

Turner sputtered, which made Raven laugh. He could tell Turner wasn't happy and that he was worried, but at least he was distracted. It was all Raven could ask for.

"Come on inside," Gallagher said. "Julian and Kaspar are visiting, and Josiah and Luther are here, too. They brought the rest of Luther's team. Some of those humans are cute."

And they wouldn't know what hit them.

It was good to see the carriers interacting with other people. Some of the humans were clearly awkward around them, probably because they weren't used to men getting pregnant. One of them couldn't seem to look away from Misha, who looked just as interested. Raven wondered if there could be something there, but it was none of his business, even if that was the case. Besides, he suspected Misha had other things to think about, considering he was about to give birth. There was no way he could stay pregnant much longer.

Raven stayed with the little group for a few hours, but he was uncomfortable. Turner had lightened up and seemingly forgotten the conversation they'd been having, but Raven knew that wasn't true. Besides, even if Turner *had* managed to forget about it, there was no way Raven could. Every time he thought about it, he remembered how he'd betrayed Turner and how hurt Turner would be when he found out. It was a terrible sensation, and Raven wasn't sure how to deal with it.

The only thing he could do was to stay with Turner for as long as Turner would permit him to. He was already losing Turner, but he still had a little time.

But not much. Not enough.

CHAPTER ELEVEN

Turner heard the vibration before Raven. He ducked under Raven's punch, twirled around, and kicked Raven right on the ass.

Raven froze and blinked at Turner. Turner grinned, then gestured at Raven's backpack next to the mats. "Your phone's ringing," he said.

"That was good," Raven said as he stepped off the mats to grab the phone.

Turner was surprised he'd managed to get so close to Raven that he'd kicked his ass. He wouldn't have been able to in any normal circumstance, which reinforced his belief that something was wrong with Raven. There wasn't much he could do about it, unfortunately. As long as Raven refused to talk, what was Turner supposed to do?

"It's Jasper," Raven said.

That got Turner's attention. "What does he want?"

Raven shook his head and answered.

As far as Turner knew, it was the first time Jasper had called Raven. He'd texted him that first time to tell them his father was planning on taking over the council, and a few times after that, but he'd never called. The fact that he was doing so now didn't bode well, or maybe it did. Turner didn't know what it meant, and he didn't like it.

"Jasper," Raven said.

"Something's about to happen," Jasper answered so loudly that even Turner could hear it.

Raven looked alarmed and strode toward the exit. Turner

didn't hesitate before following him. If Raven thought he was going to stay back, he didn't know Turner well.

"What's going on?" Raven asked as soon as he was outside the gym.

"I don't know. Something's about to happen, though."

"Are you sure?"

"I wouldn't be calling you if I weren't."

"Calm down and tell me what's going on."

Raven removed the phone from his ear and tapped on the screen. Turner was surprised that when he next heard Jasper, the phone was on speaker.

"I don't know exactly. I just heard him talking, and whatever they're planning, it's going to happen today."

"You have to give us more than that."

"I don't have anything more," Jasper yelled. "Aren't you listening to me?"

"I am, but unfortunately, there's little we can do if we don't have more information. We don't know what your father and his friends are planning, so we can't intervene."

Jasper sucked in a breath. "Okay, okay. Let me think. He was talking about the badgers. I think they're planning on attacking."

"Why the badgers?"

"How should I know? I just know what I heard, and he said something about the cete's defense system. Can you do anything?"

Raven and Turner looked at each other. "We can get to Rhodes before he does anything," Turner said.

Raven shook his head. "We can't act on our own. We need to get to Thomas."

"Not yet," Turner complained.

Raven looked at him with wide eyes. "You can't be seriously telling me you don't think it's time to talk to Thomas. I know you want to do this on your own, Turner, but that time is over. Don't be an idiot."

Turner glared. "I'm not an idiot."

"Not usually, no, but you've been behaving like one."

"Stop insulting me."

Raven sucked in a breath. "Fine. I'll stop telling you that you're being an idiot when you stop behaving like one. Is that fine with you?"

Turner glared. "You're not listening to me."

"I think you're the one who's not listening. You have to stop this, Turner." He turned his attention back to the phone call. "Thanks for telling us," he told Jasper. "Turner and I are headed to Thomas's house. We'll tell him what's going on."

"You have to hurry," Jasper said. He sounded scared, which made Turner wonder what was going on. It wasn't like Jasper to be scared. Although, considering they were dealing with his father, maybe it did make sense.

"Call us if anything else happens," Turner ordered.

"You better save me if my father gets his hands on me," Jasper said.

"We will," Raven promised. He hung up and looked at Turner. "We're going to Thomas's house."

"I'd better go to the Bishop house," Turner said. He didn't want to talk to Thomas. He didn't want to have to explain what he and Raven had hidden from the alpha. Thomas would be disappointed, and Turner didn't want to deal with that.

"You're trying to get out of it," Raven accused.

"I have things to do."

"Like what? Sneaking out and killing Rhodes on your own?"

Turner crossed his arms over his chest. "I thought you trusted me."

"I did until you went back on your promise. If you're afraid to face Thomas because of what you hid from him, you can stop. I already talked to him, as well as to Alex and the team."

The breath whooshed out of Turner's lungs, and he stared at Raven. "What did you do?" he asked.

Raven looked away. "You heard me. Thomas already knew what you were planning. That's why he asked me to train you. He knew you were going to try to kill Rhodes, and he didn't want you to do it. He asked me to keep an eye on you, and I did."

"That's why you're training me? To keep an eye on me?" Was that also why Raven had started dating Turner?

Suddenly, Turner couldn't breathe.

"It was in the beginning. I wasn't sure about it, especially because it gave you the means to do it, but Thomas insisted. I didn't expect to fall in love with you, Turner."

Turner shook his head. "I can't believe this. Was it also Thomas who told you to go along when I asked you to help me? Does he know we were spying on Rhodes?"

"He does, but because I told him, not because he asked me to do it. He wasn't happy when I explained what we'd been up to."

"You told him even though I asked you not to do it," Turner said slowly.

"I had to," Raven said.

He sounded desperate, and Turner wanted to hit him. How dare Raven be hurt? He was the one who'd gone behind Turner's back. He was the one who'd betrayed Turner. He shouldn't be in pain.

Turner shook his head. "I don't have time to deal with this right now." He turned around, having every intention of finding Rhodes and getting rid of him before he could hurt anyone. He might be pissed at Raven, but that wouldn't be a problem because he had to stop thinking about the man. He needed to focus on Rhodes, and that was what he'd do. He could nurse his broken heart once this was over.

"Where are you going?" Raven asked, catching Turner's arm and pulling him back.

Turner tried to shake him off. When Raven didn't let go, Turner turned around and punched him.

Raven jerked back, but he kept his hold on Turner. Turner moved to punch him again, but Raven was expecting it now. He caught Turner's arm and pulled him against his chest. Turner tried to get out of the embrace, but Raven wouldn't let go.

"Listen to me," Raven said.

Turner tried to hit him again. He stomped his foot on Raven's, and Raven let go. Turner wasn't done with him. He was angry, and there was no one else to take his anger out on apart from Raven.

Turner punched Raven. He half expected Raven to allow him to do what he wanted, but Raven fought back. He was lethal in a way Turner had never seen him. That was when Turner realized that even though the training had been harsh, Raven had always gone easy on him. Now, he wasn't, and Turner barely managed to get a punch in, let alone bring Raven to his knees.

Raven didn't have a problem doing it to Turner.

It took just a few moments for Turner to end up panting on the ground. Raven was standing over him, glaring at him.

"Are you done?" he asked.

"You betrayed me," Turner spat out.

"I didn't want to, but I had no choice. Look at you. How can anyone trust you not to do something stupid when it's the first thing you do when you find out Rhodes is planning something?"

It was like being punched again. "You don't trust me?"

"I trust you with everything else, but I can't with this. You don't think clearly when Rhodes is involved, and you know it. Please. I don't want to fight with you."

Turner shook his head and got to his feet. "It's too late for that. You should have thought about it before you betrayed me."

"You have to see I didn't have a choice. You have to understand I'm only doing this because you didn't leave me a choice."

But Turner *didn't* understand that. He'd trusted Raven, and Raven had betrayed him, just like everyone always had.

Raven couldn't remember the last time he'd felt so many mixed emotions. He was pissed, panicking, worried, and he didn't know what to do about any of it. He wanted to pull Turner into his arms and make him see why he'd gone to Thomas. He wanted Turner to understand that he hadn't gone into this wanting to betray him, but that he'd done it because he had to. The problem was that he doubted Turner would listen to him. He wasn't listening to anything Raven had to say, which didn't bode well.

This was the worst thing that could have happened. It was the worst way this situation could have ended, and Raven didn't know how to deal with it. He didn't even know if he *could* deal with it. He had to get to Thomas and tell him Rhodes was planning on attacking the cete, and he had to do it as soon as possible. He didn't have the time to try to make up with Turner and soothe Turner's pain, no matter how much he wanted to.

"We don't have time to talk about this right now," he said through gritted teeth.

Turner continued glaring. "Then it's good I don't want to talk about it. Actually, I never want to talk to you ever again."

It was like getting punched, but Raven schooled his expression. Turner knew he was hurting him. There was no need for everyone else around them to understand that.

"We have to go to Thomas *now*," Raven said.

"I'm not going anywhere with you."

"And what will you do, then? Go kill Rhodes on your own? Do you really think I'll allow you to do that?"

Turner's expression told Raven he was going to be stubborn. "I'm going to do what I have to do."

But he didn't understand that Raven couldn't allow that to happen. He couldn't let Turner put himself in danger, and it didn't matter if Turner hated him by the time this was over. He was pretty sure Turner already hated him, anyway.

When Turner started to turn away, Raven swooped in. He folded himself in half, pressed his shoulder against Turner's stomach, and hauled him onto his shoulder. Turner squeaked and tried to get away, but Raven wasn't letting go.

He was never letting go if he had a choice.

He doubted he would, but he'd already known this would happen. He'd known he'd lose Turner the entire time, yet it wouldn't stop him from keeping Turner safe.

Turner punched Raven. He insulted him. He tried to kick him. He did everything he could to get Raven to let him go, but Raven didn't care how many bruises he'd have by the time this was over. He carried Turner to Thomas's house, ignoring the way everyone they walked past stared. He didn't care, and at the moment, he doubted Turner did, either.

Turner was making enough noise that someone came to Thomas's door before Raven even reached it. Alex opened and blinked at them, but thankfully, he didn't ask what was going on. Raven walked right in, headed to Thomas's office.

"You should come with us," he called out over his shoulder.

He heard Alex's footsteps behind them, so he knew Alex was following.

"What's going on?" Alex asked as Raven walked into Thomas's office.

Raven finally put Turner on his feet. Turner tried to punch him, but Raven caught his punch and twisted his arm around until Turner's back was against his chest and he was pinning both of Turner's arms with his.

"Please, try to understand," he begged, not even caring that Alex and Thomas were there, listening to them. "I'm trying to keep you safe. You saw how easily I beat you just moments ago. What do you think will happen if you face Rhodes on your own?"

"I hate you," Turner spat out.

Raven's heart broke. "Maybe you do, but I love you, and I can't watch you kill yourself."

Turner tensed. Raven had expected him to try to hit him again, but instead, he stayed silent and still. Raven wished he hadn't told Turner he loved him in this situation, but at least he had, and Turner was listening to him now.

"I wish things were different, but they're not. I thought I could convince you to change your mind and for us to really work together, but I know you've always planned on killing Rhodes on your own," Raven explained. "Yes, I lied to you, but you lied to me, too. I hope we'll manage to come back from this, but if we can't, if you can't forgive me, then remember I did it because I care."

Turner pushed away from Raven, and Raven allowed him to move this time. Now that he'd told Turner everything he'd wanted to say, it was time to focus on the problem at hand.

He straightened and looked at Thomas and Alex, who were watching them. "Jasper called. He thinks his father is going to attack the cete today."

Alex swore, but Thomas didn't look surprised. "I suppose he feels it's my fault that things changed so much in the forest lately," he said.

"Do you know anything else?" Alex asked Raven.

"No. I don't even know when it's going to happen exactly.

I just know it will and that we need to be ready. We can't plan anything and try to stop this before it happens because we don't know who's going to be here and when they'll arrive. We need to gather everyone, though."

Thomas reached for his phone. He started making phone calls, and Raven tried to relax. It was out of his hands now. People who knew better than he did how to do this were in charge, and it was a relief.

He peeked at Turner, who was ignoring him and staring out the window instead. He didn't know what to do with Turner, or even if he could do anything to fix things. It would have to wait.

There would be nothing to fix if Rhodes attacked the cete and won. There would be nothing to fix if Turner snuck out and went to Rhodes on his own. Raven had to protect Turner and the cete, and only once he'd succeeded would he be able to focus on his personal life. It was going to be hell, but he could do it.

He had to.

Turner was out of place. He was still seething, but he wanted to be involved in whatever was going on. The problem was that he wasn't.

He didn't belong in this room. He wasn't an alpha—just the thought it was ridiculous—and he didn't work with pack security. Thomas and Raven had humored him for a while, but that was clearly over, and they weren't even looking at him now. He understood they had other things to focus on, but what was he supposed to do? Just stand there and wait for the adults to make decisions? Turner was twenty-seven, for fuck's sake. He might be a carrier, but he was still a man, and he wanted the people in this room to treat him like one instead of like an unruly child.

"Morris is sending people," Thomas said as he hung up the phone. "He said he'd contact the deer, so we won't have to do it."

Alex nodded. "We should head to the border of our territory. There are only a few spots where Rhodes can come in, and we should be able to secure them. I already contacted my team, and even though most of them aren't badgers, they're coming."

"I want to be there, too," Turner intervened.

Raven opened his mouth, no doubt to tell Turner no, but before he could speak, Thomas did.

"You're not going anywhere," he said softly.

Turner stiffened his back. "This is my fight, too."

"You have every right to be angry at Rhodes and want to kill him, but you're not leaving this house, Turner. I'm sorry. I understand you're angry at me, and you might even hate me. You might decide to leave the Bishop house and the cete once this is over because you can't stand to talk to me ever again. I wouldn't be happy with that, but I'd understand. I'm the alpha, though, and as long as you live in badger territory, you'll listen to me. You're not up to facing Rhodes, even with the training Raven has been putting you through. Besides, even if you were, I wouldn't let you come with us. You're too angry, and angry men make bad decisions. I can't have you risk your life and the lives of others."

"I might not be as well trained as Raven and the other guards, but it doesn't mean I'm useless," Turner protested.

He could hear the hint of begging in his voice, but at this point, he didn't care. He needed to go out there with the others. He needed to be part of this, to watch Rhodes as he was killed. He didn't even care if he was the one to kill him at this point. He just wanted the man to die.

Thomas shook his head. "You'll stay here, in this house. A few of your friends are visiting with Joel, and they'll keep an eye on you."

"You can't treat me like a child," Turner snapped.

"Then stop acting like one. You're not rational, not over this, and I don't think you ever will be. I don't blame you for it, but this is an order, Turner. You'll stay in this house, and you won't try to get to Rhodes. You won't like the consequences if you disobey."

Thomas was apparently done talking to Turner. He got to his feet and strode to the door, leaning out. "Joel?" he called out.

It took Joel a moment to get there. Before he did, Turner tried to find another way to convince Thomas to allow him to go with them, but he knew he wouldn't succeed.

It was the first time Thomas had done something like this. It was the first time he sounded so harsh and angry at Turner, and Turner didn't like it.

He didn't like not being able to get to Rhodes even more.

He never wanted to lose the cete. It had become his home when he didn't have one, and not coming back would hurt almost as much as losing Raven. There was no way Turner wouldn't try to get out of the house if he could, though. He was ready to face whatever punishment Thomas believed was right when this was over, but in the meantime, he wouldn't think about it. He'd focus on getting to Rhodes and giving the man everything he deserved for what he'd done to him and other carriers.

Turner was doing this, and it didn't matter that Raven and Thomas weren't okay with it.

Joel appeared at the open office door. He looked around, instantly understand something was going on. "What do you need from me?" he asked his father.

"To keep an eye on Turner."

Joel's eyes widened, and he looked at Turner. "What happened?"

Turner shook his head. He might have decided he'd do this anyway, but it didn't mean he wanted to tell his friend.

Turner didn't want to lose Joel, the carriers at the Bishop house, or the cete, but he'd decided a long time ago that killing Rhodes would be worth losing that and more. It would be worth losing his life if that was what happened.

"We'll explain later," Thomas said. "Just know that someone is about to attack the cete, so I need you and your mother to stay inside the house. Keep the carriers here, too, especially Turner."

Joel's eyes widened in alarm, but he nodded, ready to obey his father. "Of course. Be careful."

Thomas smiled and patted Joel's shoulder. "Always. The same goes for you."

Joel turned his attention to Turner. "Let's go. We should head upstairs."

Turner looked around, trying to find someone who would change their mind. Thomas had already dismissed him, though, and he was talking to Alex. Raven looked like his heart had been broken, and Turner took a savage satisfaction in it for a moment. Then he remembered his heart was just as broken as Raven's, and he felt awful.

Raven wasn't going to help him. He'd made what he thought of Turner and the situation clear. So Turner turned to Joel and followed him out the door.

"Do you want to tell me what happened?" Joel asked.

Turner shook his head. "I don't want to talk about it."

"Well, whatever it was, just know that my father only wants what's best for you."

Turner snorted. "He's treating me like a child."

"Have you thought that maybe it's his right to do it? Because my father isn't a mean man, and he's not a cruel alpha. I don't think he'd treat you unfairly, which tells me something happened."

Turner glared. "He just thinks I'm weak because I'm a carrier." But the words didn't sound right anymore.

Joel shook his head. "That's not the case, and you know it. You know my father, Turner. I have no idea why you're denying the truth, even to yourself, but maybe you should think about it and about the reason my father wanted me to keep an eye on you."

Turner pressed his lips together. He didn't want to fight with Joel, and he could tell that was where they were headed. It was better for him not to say anything else, and he stayed silent as he followed Joel into the living room and found several of the guys that he lived with there. Misha wasn't, which was a relief. The Bishop house was deep inside cete territory, so there was no way Rhodes would get to it. He'd have to kill every single badger before he could, and that wasn't going to happen.

Turner settled on the chair next to the door and crossed his arms over his chest. A few of his friends tried to pull him into their conversation, but he limited himself to grunts, and they soon stopped. He kept listening, trying to find out what was going on in the office, but the only thing he could hear were voices. He had no idea what was happening, and that made him angry again.

He forced himself to think about the situation. Both Raven and Thomas had told him that he couldn't think straight when Rhodes was involved, and he couldn't deny it was true. When he thought about what his old alpha had done to him, he wanted to scream and get his hands on the man, do to him what he'd done to Turner. He wasn't stupid, and he did realize that having that level of anger wasn't good when facing someone who could easily kill you.

So yes, Thomas and Raven were right. Turner wasn't thinking straight, and he'd probably have made a mistake if he'd faced Rhodes on his own.

That wasn't going to stop Turner. He stood to lose everything, but it didn't matter. He'd get to Rhodes, and he'd have
his revenge, even if it killed him.

And, to be honest—it probably would.

Raven kept peeking at the door, but Turner didn't come back.
He wouldn't, not after Thomas had told him to go. Turner had
been angry but also heartbroken, and seeing that expression
on his face had broken Raven's heart, too.

What was left of it, anyway.

Raven had known that if he betrayed Turner and talked to
Thomas behind his back, he'd lose him, but he'd done it anyway. He'd do it again, too, if it meant Turner was safe. Raven
could live without having Turner in his life as long as he knew
Turner was alive and safe somewhere.

Or at least, he hoped so.

"Raven?" Thomas said.

Raven shook himself. No matter how much he wanted to
focus on Turner, go after him and apologize again, make sure
Turner forgave him, he couldn't. Turner was safe for the moment, but he wouldn't stay safe if Rhodes had his way.

"Yes?" Raven asked.

"You think you can call Jasper again? We need to know at
least part of what's going to happen, and he's the only one
who can help us."

"You're going to have to tell me how you convinced him
eventually," Alex intervened. "I can't believe he's been working against his father with you."

"That tells you everything you need to know about Alpha
Rhodes, doesn't it?" Raven answered as he took his phone out
of his pocket.

He quickly unlocked the screen and found Jasper's number. He called, but Jasper didn't answer, and Raven started to

worry. Had Rhodes found out what his son was doing? Had he gotten rid of Jasper so he wouldn't be able to help the badgers?

"Raven?" Jasper answered the second time Raven called.

Raven's knees went weak with relief. "I thought something had happened to you," he said.

"I'm surprised nothing has yet," Jasper told him. "What's going on? Are you with Thomas?"

"I am. Alex is here, too, and they've been making phone calls. We'll be ready for your father when he arrives, but we need to know more about what's going on."

"I knew you'd be calling again, so I stuck around."

"Does your father know?"

"I wouldn't be talking to you if he did. A large group of shifters arrived about half an hour ago. They're all dressed for a fight, so I think that whatever they've been planning, it's going to happen in the next few hours."

"How large is the group?"

"I counted about twenty people, but a few more cars have arrived since then, so it's going to be more. Right now, I think there are about thirty. I think that's all of them, but I can't know for sure."

"That's fine. Just tell us everything you can." It would have to be enough.

"Well, I recognized a few of those guys. It's nothing good, but then, I don't suppose you expected anything good to come out of this."

He started giving Raven names, and Raven wrote all of them down. He wasn't surprised at most of the ones he recognized.

"I'll continue keeping an eye on them," Jasper said. "I—" Jasper cried out, and the phone made a noise as if it had been dropped.

"Jasper?" Raven asked. His heart raced because he knew

something had happened. "Jasper?" he called out again.

He heard the phone move, and he held his breath, waiting for Jasper to say something.

Instead, whoever had taken the phone hung up.

Raven lowered his and looked at Thomas and Alex. "Something happened to him."

"We need to do something," Thomas said. "Raven, do you think you can take care of it?"

"I should be here and defend the cete."

"We can do without you, but you're the one who brought Jasper into this, and it wouldn't be right for you to abandon him now. We have no way to know what happened to him, but if something did, we need to intervene."

Raven nodded. He didn't like the thought of leaving the cete when they most needed him, but he was only one man. They'd manage without him, especially since other shifter groups were sending their people to help.

"I'll go alone," he declared.

"I don't think that's a good idea."

"But I know how to sneak into skunk territory. I know where Jasper's house is, and I'm sure I can get in and out without anyone seeing me."

Thomas considered Raven's offer. "We won't be able to help you if something happens to you while you're in skunk territory," he warned.

"I realize that, and I'm ready to deal with the consequences. But Rhodes is coming here. Even if he found his son and knocked him out, I don't think he'll bring Jasper along." Hopefully, Rhodes had just knocked his son out instead of killing him, but Raven wouldn't put it past him.

"Be careful," Thomas ordered. "We don't know when Rhodes will attack, which means he's still in skunk territory at the moment. Don't do anything rash or stupid, and make sure no one sees you."

"I'll do everything I can," Raven promised.

"And if you can't get to Jasper without putting yourself in danger or getting hurt, don't even try. I want to help him as much as you do, but I won't sacrifice you for that. If there are too many people around and you can't help him yourself, call me, and I'll send a team to help."

Raven hoped he wouldn't need that help. The cete needed everyone to stay here and be ready to defend it from Rhodes when he arrived. They could spare one man, maybe two, but no more. Raven could do this on his own, no matter what he had to face when he got in skunk territory.

"I'll let you know," he promised.

Thomas nodded and squeezed Raven's arm. "Be careful, please. I don't want to lose you, and I know Turner doesn't, either."

Raven grimaced. "I'm pretty sure he'd dance on my grave at the moment."

"He's angry. You and I know you've done the right thing, and I think Turner will understand that if he takes the time to think about it. It might take him a while, but he'll come around."

Hope bloomed in Raven's chest. He didn't know if Thomas was right, but he supposed only the future would tell. For that to happen, though, both he and Turner had to have a future, which meant Raven needed to be careful and make sure both of them made it out of this alive.

He had every intention of doing just that.

Chapter Twelve

Turner could hear Thomas, Alex, and Raven getting ready to leave. People were running around the house, and the tension was high.

And Turner was barred from it, like a child who'd misbehaved.

He'd be the first to admit he hadn't gone about this the right way. He and Raven should have talked to Thomas sooner, and it was his fault they hadn't. He hated being kept out of things, though. This was his fight, too, and it wasn't fair that he couldn't be part of it. But Thomas had ordered him to stay here, and Turner knew the punishment for disobeying his alpha.

He was going to do it anyway.

He'd have to wait until most of the people were out of the house. There was no way he could sneak out while Thomas and the others were still there, but when only Thomas's wife and the carriers were left? Turner wouldn't hesitate. He couldn't, not when this would be his only chance to get to Rhodes.

So he stayed where he was, and he listened. He ignored how the others kept watching him as if they were afraid he was about to explode. They weren't wrong. He felt like he was, and he couldn't act as if that wasn't the case. They already knew he was pissed, so he kept his gaze forward and his chin in a stubborn expression no one was surprised to see on him.

"This is scary," Gallagher said.

Turner had to remind himself that Gallagher's situation had been worse than his. Almost everyone's situation in the Bishop house had been worse, yet, they weren't trying to kill anyone.

"You're sure you don't want to talk about it?" Joel asked as he passed by Turner.

Turner shook his head. "There's nothing to talk about."

"From what you told me, that's not true."

"What do you want me to say? They're treating me as if I'm nothing more than a child. I hate it."

"I don't know what happened, but I don't think my father would have treated you like that if he didn't have a good reason."

Turner scowled. "So you're saying it's my fault."

"Maybe? You don't want to tell me, so I don't know. Just remember that I'm here if you want to talk about it. We all are, and you don't have to sit there on your own."

Turner shook his head and looked away. The next time he glanced in Joel's direction, Joel was gone.

From the lack of sound, he wasn't the only one. The house appeared mostly empty by now, which was exactly what Turner had been waiting for. He didn't go right away, even though he desperately wanted to. Instead, he remained a moment longer, watching the carriers in the living room.

They were talking to each other, their heads close, and they looked like a family. He could be part of that family, but he'd always felt a bit outside of it. He realized it was his own fault. He hoped that once this was over, he could be closer to his friends. He'd been focused on killing Rhodes so much so that he'd isolated himself from the people he considered family. He'd told himself it was because he wanted them to be safe. Once Rhodes was gone, they would be, and Turner could finally start living his life.

Provided that he stayed alive.

He wasn't sure how long he waited, but once he was sure no one was coming back, he gave the carriers in the living room one last glance. They were still talking, and no one was paying attention to him. It was the perfect moment to sneak out, so he did. He got to his feet, relieved his chair didn't creak, and slipped out of the door. Once in the hallway, he waited a moment longer, just to make sure no one had noticed he wasn't there anymore. When no one called out for him or told him to come back, he left.

Since he'd been sent away, he wasn't sure what Rhodes was planning and whether Thomas and the others had found out. He couldn't wait for Rhodes to come into badger territory, because if he did, it would be too late for him to take care of him. That meant he had to go to Rhodes in skunk territory.

He hadn't been there on his own since he'd first left. The few times he'd gone back, Raven had been with him, and Turner had been relieved. He'd needed Raven, and he felt he still did, even though he hated it.

He didn't want to need Raven or anyone else, but especially not Raven, who had betrayed him. Turner wasn't sure they could ever come back from that. He hoped so, but he wouldn't find out until this was over.

He left the house and looked around. He couldn't walk to skunk territory, and he didn't have a car. That meant he was going to have to steal one of the cars parked in front of the house.

He grinned when he saw Raven's. It was petty, but at the moment, he didn't care. He didn't know why Raven hadn't taken his car, but he should have.

Like everyone else in his cete, Raven never took the keys out of their car when they parked. It wouldn't have made sense, not when no one would steal them. That meant that Turner didn't even have to worry he wouldn't be able to start the car. The keys were in the ignition, and he just had to turn them.

Turner drove away. He looked back at the house one last time to see that Joel was standing in front of it, having heard the car. He'd no doubt call his father, and Turner hoped he'd be far away by the time Thomas managed to do anything. He felt a bit guilty, because Thomas should focus on keeping the cete safe, but that was what Turner was doing, too. If Rhodes weren't a part of this, everyone would be safe.

He drove out of badger territory, or at least, he tried to. He didn't get far, because when he reached the main road, he saw a group of cars coming toward him in the distance. He stopped the car and stared, wondering who it was and hoping it was help coming.

The problem was that he couldn't be sure.

It could be the bears, the deer, or anyone else who'd agreed to help, but it could also be Rhodes and his friends. Turner bit his lower lip and stayed where he was, staring until he saw who was sitting in the car's passenger seat.

Rhodes.

Turner was too late.

He didn't know what to do. His first instinct was to run back to Raven so he'd be safe, but he hated himself for thinking that. He knew he couldn't beat all of these people on his own, but maybe he could do what he could to slow them down. He had his phone, so after moving the car into the middle of the road, he took it out and texted Raven to tell him that Rhodes was coming.

Then he left his phone on the passenger seat and got out of the car to face his destiny.

Raven almost didn't check his phone when he felt it vibrating in his pocket. The only reason he did was that he was still hoping Jasper would call him back since he hadn't been able to leave yet. Anyone else would know to call Thomas or his beta, or even Alex.

Raven took his phone out of his pocket anyway, and his heart stopped, reading the text that had arrived.

"Turner is gone, and Rhodes is here," he said with a gasp.

There were several ways to get in badger territory, and he, Thomas, and Alex were at one of the roads. Apparently, it wasn't the one Rhodes had chosen.

Thomas was next to Raven in seconds. "What happened?"

"I don't know. I just got a text from Turner that he left the house, and he's blocking the road from Rhodes and the others arriving with him."

Thomas swore, something he didn't often do. "That means they're not coming in through here."

"Unless they separated," Alex said in a worried tone.

Thomas nodded and started pointing at people. "The five of you, stay here. Let us know if anyone tries to come in. The rest, with me."

He didn't have to repeat himself. People followed him when he started running, and since Thomas hadn't told Raven to stay, he went along. He wouldn't have stayed, even if Thomas had ordered him to.

What had Turner been thinking? How could he be away from Thomas's house when Thomas had ordered him to stay where he was? What would Thomas do to him once this was over?

Raven was almost afraid to find out, and he reminded himself that before worrying about what would happen after Rhodes had been taken care of, they actually needed to take care of him.

"Did he tell you anything else?" Thomas asked as they ran.

"Just that he left the house and was taking the most direct road out of cete territory."

"I didn't think Rhodes would have the balls to come in through that road. I should have known better."

And Raven should have known better than to expect Turner to stay where he was. He was so angry and focused on getting to Rhodes himself that it wasn't a surprise. Turner should have respected Thomas enough to obey his orders, but he was blinded by revenge and hatred. The only way to keep him inside the house would have been to tie him up, and Raven suspected he would have found a way out anyway. He prayed Turner wasn't doing something stupid, but he knew that probably wasn't the case. Turner had texted that he was blocking the road, which meant he'd put himself in Rhodes's path.

He was going to get himself killed, but if he didn't, Raven would kill him himself — right after kissing him.

Raven didn't think he'd ever run so fast. It still didn't feel fast enough, and he knew he was right when he finally saw his car blocking the road. Of course Turner had taken his car. The little shit would have done anything he had to in order to get to Rhodes, including walking there. He hadn't needed to, because Rhodes had come to him instead.

Turner had parked Raven's car in the middle of the road so the cars arriving couldn't get past it, but one had hit Raven's car straight on, twisting it to the side. That car was still there on the side of the road, smoke coming out of it. The others were gone, except for one more, and Raven knew who it belonged to. The owner wasn't in the car but out of it, standing on the road and fighting with Turner.

Rhodes laughed and grabbed Turner as Turner threw himself at him. He twisted around and hurled Turner to the side, still laughing. Even though Raven couldn't see Turner's expression, he knew how Turner felt. He'd never taken it well when people laughed of him, and even though Raven wasn't anywhere near close enough, he heard the cry of hatred that came out of Turner when he landed on his knees.

It wasn't enough to stop Turner. He got back to his feet,

moved into a fighting position, and stepped toward Rhodes again.

"Dammit," Raven swore.

"The others have gone straight to my house," Thomas said. "We have to get to them."

"Go. I'll make sure Rhodes doesn't join you."

"He's not the only one there." Two guys were waiting by Rhodes's car, and they'd seen Raven and the others. They looked hesitant, no doubt because they knew they couldn't take their entire group on their own. "Calder?" Thomas asked.

Calder nodded and stepped next to Raven. "Raven and I will take care of those."

"Remember, you still have to go to Jasper," Thomas told Raven.

Raven wanted to go now, but the cete was his family and home. He needed to make sure they were protected before he could think of anyone else. "I'll go as soon as these guys have been taken care of."

Thomas nodded. "Be careful. All of you."

They separated, and Raven started moving toward Rhodes. Rhodes wasn't laughing anymore, not since Turner had punched him in the face. Rhodes was bleeding, and he looked pissed.

Raven was surprised to see that Turner was actually holding his own. He was bleeding, too, from a deep cut in his lower lip, but it hadn't stopped him. It didn't look like it had even slowed him down. He was still standing, and now that he wasn't letting anger drive him, he was getting in more hits than Raven had expected. It was obvious Rhodes hadn't expected it, either, and he was having a hard time dealing with it.

Turner darted forward, aiming his fist at Rhodes's face. Rhodes moved to block him, but Turner never had any intention of punching him. When Rhodes moved, he moved, too, lowering himself and kicking at Rhodes's knee. It buckled, and Rhodes swayed. Turner took the opportunity to hit him again, in the face this time.

Raven was impressed, but that didn't mean he was going to let Turner get himself killed. He started moving toward Rhodes, knowing Calder would take care of the two guys staring, but before he could get there, a hand on his shoulder stopped him.

"You have to let him do this on his own," Calder said.

"He's not a guard."

"It doesn't seem to me like he has to be one to hold his own. He's doing well, and I'm afraid those two guys are going to slip away if we don't intervene."

"He's going to get hurt."

"And it will be his choice. He knows what he's doing, Raven. You can't continue protecting him, not when he's the one who left the house and threw himself into danger. Be there for him if he needs you, but let him to do this if he doesn't. He needs it."

Calder was right. No matter how much Raven wanted to go to Turner's rescue, Turner wouldn't thank him for it. He already hated him, and doing that would make everything worse.

Even though it was the hardest thing he'd ever done, Raven took a step back and turned his attention to the two guys who'd been hovering by the car.

He had to remember that he'd trained Turner and that while Turner wasn't a guard and didn't have as much experience as Raven, he could defend himself. He was showing it right now, holding his own against Rhodes. He could continue doing so while Raven and Calder took care of the other two guys, and maybe he could even beat Rhodes.

And wouldn't that be a nice thing to see? Rhodes had come

here convinced he'd beat the cete and kill Thomas, take over the council, and rule over the forest. Instead, he'd been stopped by one of the people he believed was weak, by one of the men he'd imprisoned and treated like shit.

Raven wasn't a spiritual man, but he thought there was beauty in that.

He moved toward the car and the men standing there. Part of his attention was still on Turner and Rhodes, but that wouldn't be a problem. He cracked his knuckles as he reached the men, and they looked even more hesitant. They clearly weren't fighters, and he couldn't imagine why Rhodes had wanted them to come. Where had he found these people?

Not that it mattered. Whoever they were, whatever reason they were here for, they wouldn't leave this place in one piece.

Raven threw himself at the closest man. The man squeaked and tried to scramble to the car, but Raven grabbed him by the back of the shirt and pulled him back. The fight was on, and while he couldn't wait for it to be over so he could check on Turner, he had faith in the man he loved.

Turner knew Raven was there. He'd seen him from the corner of his eye. Part of him wanted to ask Raven for help, to bury himself in Raven's arms and allow Raven to take care of him. Another part of him wanted to show Raven how strong he was and that he'd been right in doing what he'd done. Yet another part just wanted to forget about all of this. Forget about Rhodes, the fight, what Raven had done to him, and what he'd done to Raven. He just wanted to snuggle into Raven's arms and forget about everything.

He wouldn't be able to do that until Rhodes was taken care of.

Turner had been at first surprised that he'd been able to hit Rhodes as many times as he had. He'd expected his old alpha to wipe the floor with him and leave him in a bloody heap, but instead, Turner had the upper hand. All the training Raven had put him through was working. It wasn't perfect, and Turner knew he'd end up with bruises by the end of the day, but he didn't care. They'd be worth seeing the expression on Rhodes's face when Turner had managed to hit him that first time.

No matter how much Turner wanted to focus on Raven, he couldn't look away from Rhodes right now.

He'd just hit the alpha on the knee, and it looked like Rhodes was in pain every time he took a step. He was trying hard not to let it show, but Turner could read him. He'd taught himself to when he was a child because he'd wanted to be able to tell when Rhodes was angry and when it would be better to stay away from the alpha, and he was glad to see he remembered most of Rhodes's expressions. Rhodes was pissed, but there was also a hint of fear and uncertainty in the way he looked at Turner.

"So this is what you've been doing?" Rhodes asked. "I thought Thomas would have been smarter. He should have known that the only way you can repay him for his kindness is on your back."

Turner's first instinct was to scream and attack. Instead, he sucked in a breath. "Thomas sees things you can't see," he said through gritted teeth.

"Like what? I just don't think you're his type. Doesn't mean he won't force you to open your legs soon, though. That's all you people are good for."

Turner was going to kick Rhodes's ass and make sure he remembered who had done it.

But this was good. Even though Turner was keeping up with Rhodes, Rhodes still believed Turner was weak. That meant he wasn't paying too much attention when he really should have been.

Turner couldn't allow the anger to take over. Raven and Thomas were right when they'd said that was all Turner was focused on when he thought of Rhodes. If he let his anger win, so would Rhodes. He'd take advantage of it, which was what he was trying to do.

But Turner knew better. He would win this fight, and he'd make sure everyone remembered it.

He circled Rhodes, avoiding a few swipes Rhodes gave his way. Rhodes didn't look like he was trying very hard, but Turner wasn't sure if it was because he was trying to understand how strong Turner was or because he truly believed Turner was weaker than him and that it would be easy to beat him.

He should know better by now.

"Just stay still," Rhodes said with a growl. "I'll end this soon, and you can go back where you belong."

Turner snorted. "And where is that? Barefoot and pregnant in the kitchen?"

"I should have kicked your ass when I had you."

"I don't think you'd have been able to, even before I started training. Let's be honest. You were never the greatest fighter." Turner patted his stomach. "If I didn't know you weren't a carrier, I'd think you were pregnant."

Rhodes roared and threw himself at Turner. Turner had expected it—had in fact hoped for it. He grabbed Rhodes's wrist and pulled him forward, unbalancing him. Rhodes swore and tried to stay on his feet by grabbing Turner, but Turner danced just out of reach and hit Rhodes in the middle of the back with both his fists. Then, before Rhodes could fall, he put all his strength into the kick to the back of his knee.

This time, Rhodes did go down. Turner didn't wait for him to get back to his feet. He straddled Rhodes's back, grabbed his head with both his hands, and slammed it on the ground. Rhodes tried to fight, but even though Turner wasn't heavily muscled, he was heavy enough that Rhodes couldn't throw him off his body.

He continued to slam Rhodes's face on the ground, ignoring the blood spraying on his hands, dripping into the earth and tingeing it red. He wanted to kill Rhodes, to make sure Rhodes didn't hurt anyone ever again. He wanted the man to suffer for what he'd done to him, and at the moment, he didn't care about anything else.

But then he froze.

His fingers were still buried in Rhodes's hair, even though he'd pulled out several strands. Blood was pooling under Rhodes's face, and even though Rhodes was still trying to push Turner off him, his movements were weak, and he kept whimpering.

Was this really what Turner wanted? What kind of person would he be if he killed Rhodes like he was tempted to?

Yes, he'd been planning to kill his old alpha since he'd been freed from that shed. He'd trained for it, planned for it, and had every intention of going through with it, at least until now.

He wasn't sure anymore.

Meeting Raven, dating him, had changed the way Turner looked at this. He still wanted his revenge, and he had it. Rhodes would always remember who had beaten him, and Turner was satisfied with that. Rhodes would spend the rest of his life behind bars, knowing Turner had been the one who put him there, just like Turner had known it was Rhodes who'd put him in that shed. Wasn't that the sweetest revenge?

Thinking that way scared Turner. He couldn't help but wonder if Rhodes would escape and come after him. It was a possibility, something he wouldn't have to worry about if he killed Rhodes. But what would happen even if Rhodes did come after him? Turner had beaten him once. He could do it again.

He didn't have to kill Rhodes to get his revenge. If anything, revenge would be sweeter when he knew that Rhodes was behind bars, thinking about him and hating him every day. Killing him wouldn't give Turner the healing he'd hoped it would, but this might.

Without noticing, he'd already started healing. He'd opened his heart to Raven and had fallen in love with him. More importantly, he'd accepted that he wasn't weak and that allowing people to care about him didn't make him so. It wouldn't always be easy, and Turner didn't think he was entirely over what Rhodes had done to him, but he was on his way, and he didn't want to ruin it by doing something stupid.

He let go of Rhodes's hair.

Rhodes's face hit the ground hard, making him groan painfully. Turner stared at him for a moment, wondering why he'd ever been afraid of the man. Rhodes had seemed so big and scary when Turner had been in that shed, but he wasn't anymore. If anything, he was pathetic. He'd hurt Turner because he thought Turner was weak, but Turner had shown him that wasn't the case. He'd shown him that even a carrier could take charge of his life and do what he wanted with it.

And what he wanted wasn't to kill Rhodes.

Turner got to his feet. Rhodes rolled to his back and tried to do the same, but even though Turner wasn't planning on killing him anymore, he wasn't letting Rhodes leave. He kicked the man in the stomach, grinning at the pained sound that came from him. He leaned closer so Rhodes could hear him over his whimpers.

"You're going to spend the rest of your life in jail," he murmured. "And every single day, you'll remember who put you behind bars. You'll remember that it was me, the man you thought was too weak to stand up to you. You were going to ruin my life, but instead, I ruined yours. And while you'll never see the light of day again, I'll be out here, happy and living my life the way I want to live it."

Turner had nothing else to tell Rhodes, and he stepped away. He doubted the alpha would get back on his feet, which was perfectly fine with him. He was done with Rhodes, and he never wanted to deal with him again. Someone else could pick up the trash.

By the time Raven and Calder were done dealing with the two guys, Turner was done with Rhodes, too. When Raven turned toward them, it was to see Rhodes flat on his front, with Turner on his back slamming his face against the ground. He'd been tempted to intervene, but just like Calder had suggested, he'd let Turner deal with it on his own. It would have been his right to kill Rhodes after what Rhodes had done to him, but Raven was relieved when he stopped.

He didn't want Turner to kill anyone, not even Rhodes. A lot of people didn't realize what an impact killing someone had until they did it, and once they had, they couldn't take it back. Raven didn't want Turner to carry that for the rest of his life.

He was glad when Turner kicked Rhodes in the stomach one last time after getting back to his feet, though.

"He did well," Calder said.

"I wasn't sure he'd stop."

"Neither was I, but I wouldn't have blamed him if he hadn't. I'm glad he did."

"So am I."

"You should take Turner and go to Jasper. I'll take care of Rhodes and make sure he doesn't get back on his feet."

Raven had almost forgotten Jasper after everything that happened, and now that Calder reminded him, he swore. "I really hope his father didn't kill him."

"Knowing what I do about Rhodes, I doubt it. If I had to

take a guess, I think he barely even hurt his son. He'd have wanted Jasper alive to show him what he'd done if he'd won."

"But he didn't."

Calder grinned. "Definitely not."

Raven wasn't sure Turner would want to go with him to rescue Jasper, but he had to ask. He moved toward the man he loved, hoping Turner would want to talk to him. Turner looked hesitant when he noticed Raven, but he didn't tell Raven to fuck off, which Raven took as a good sign.

"You did good," he said.

Turner raised his chin. "I told you I could do it."

"I never doubted that. I just didn't want anything to happen to you."

"And nothing did."

Raven looked at the cut on Turner's lip, at the way patches on his skin were already darkening. They would become bruises, but he knew Turner wouldn't have it any other way. It still hurt to see him in this state, but Raven knew better than to say that out loud. Turner was aware of how he felt, and if he wanted to forgive Raven, to understand why Raven had done what he'd done, he would.

In the meantime, they had something to do.

"We need to go to skunk territory and check in on Jasper," he said.

"Shit. I'd forgotten about him. Have you heard from him?"

"Not recently." And Raven was worried.

He hadn't known Jasper before, and he hadn't been sure what to think of the man. He still wasn't, but he couldn't deny Jasper had helped them even though it had put him in danger. Hopefully, Jasper's father hadn't killed him, but there was only one way to find out.

"I'll come with you," Turner said.

"You don't have to. I'm sure you want to head to Thomas's house and help defend the cete."

"And you'd let me?"

"I think it's clear that I wouldn't let or not let you do anything. You make your own decisions."

Turner grinned, and, for a moment, they were as they had been before. Then Turner's expression sobered. "And you better remember that," he murmured.

"I don't think I can ever forget it. We need to go, though."

"I'm ready when you are."

Raven eyed his car. "I hope it's still working."

He was delighted when Turner's cheeks turned pink. "Sorry about that."

"Don't worry. It's just a car." And Raven couldn't have cared less, not as long as Turner was okay.

They left Calder behind and scrambled into the car. Raven held his breath as he turned the key in the ignition, relieved when the car came to life. Hopefully, it would hold together long enough for them to get to skunk territory and check on Jasper. He hoped the car wouldn't stop in the middle of the road.

He drove out of badger territory with one last glance at Calder, who was on the phone, looking relaxed. Whoever he was talking to had obviously given him good news about the fight at Thomas's house. Still, Raven glanced at Turner. "Text one of the carriers who were at the house. I want to know what's going on there."

"I'm not sure any of them will want to talk to me," Turner whispered.

"Why not? What did you do?"

"I snuck out."

"Joel told me, and that's the only reason we knew to come this way. If you hadn't done it, Rhodes and his friends would have attacked the house and the carriers inside. The outcome would have been a lot worse."

Turner's fingers flew on the screen of his phone, and he

didn't look at Raven. But Raven could hear the hesitancy in his voice when he asked, "Do you think Thomas will forgive me for disobeying his order? Like you said, things would have been much worse if I hadn't."

"He's not going to kick you out of the cete, if that's what you're asking. You'll be punished, but you know him. He won't be cruel."

Turner's shoulders relaxed. "Good. Joel says that everything has been taken care of. Apparently, a few of the guys who came with Rhodes tried to run away and are wandering around cete territory, but they're not a danger."

Raven breathed out. He was relieved to hear that, and while he still wanted to go back and make sure the cete was okay, he could focus better on Jasper now.

It hadn't escaped him that Turner was acting as if they'd never fought. It was almost as if they were back to how they'd been before, and Raven hoped it would last. He was afraid to ask Turner if he'd forgiven him and terrified of the answer Turner would give him. Besides, now wasn't the right moment to do it.

"I'm sorry," Turner said after a moment.

Raven wouldn't allow himself to hope, but he still asked, "What are you apologizing for?"

"You were right when you said that I shouldn't be angry at you for lying when I did the same thing. I told you we'd go to Thomas and that I wouldn't go after Rhodes on my own, yet I had every intention of doing just that. And I did. I went after Rhodes on my own."

"And you won."

"That's not the point. When I was fighting him, I realized that you were right. I was letting my anger take over, and I would have lost if I hadn't stopped that. I actually did the same to Rhodes. I knew how to make him angry, and I did. When he snapped, he stopped thinking carefully about what he was doing, and I took advantage of that. He'd been trying to do the same, but in the end, I'm the one who won."

Raven was glad and relieved to hear that. Turner hadn't been without fault in this situation, and while Raven shouldn't have gone behind his back, he hadn't seen another way to do it. "I'm sorry, too. I should have tried harder to convince you to go to Thomas harder."

Turner snorted. "How could you have done that? You told me to go to Thomas several times. You explained why you thought we should do it, but I didn't listen. I should have. We wouldn't be in this situation if I had."

Raven held his breath. "And what situation are we in?"

"I'm not sure. I want to hate you because you betrayed me, but I understand why you did it. I was the one at fault, and you did the best you could with what I was giving you. It still hurts to know that you went behind my back, and I think it's going to hurt for a while, but I want to be able to forget it."

"You'd forgive me for betraying you?"

"You had to make a choice. You were trying to protect both me and the cete, and you did it the only way you could think of. It couldn't have been easy for you."

"It wasn't. I hated doing it, but I'd do it again if I had to. I know everything went well with Rhodes, but it might not have, and I would never have forgiven myself if he'd hurt you."

"That's why I think I'll be able to forgive you. Because I know you just wanted what was best for me, and you tried giving it to me even though I fought so hard. I can't say I'll ever thank you for it, but I think I can get over it." Turner paused. "I want *us* to get over it. I want us to go back to what we were before and go from there. Do you think we can do that?"

Raven offered Turner his hand, hoping Turner would take it. When he did, he linked their fingers together and settled both their hands on his thigh. "We'll work things out," he promised.

"There's nothing I want more."

By the time they were done with their conversation, they'd reached skunk territory. Raven almost parked where he'd hid the car before, but Turner stopped him. "You should drive right up to Jasper's house."

"Why?"

"Jasper is the new alpha. We need to show him some respect."

"As long as no one tries to intervene."

"I don't think they will."

Turner was right. Raven drove right into skunk territory, past Rhodes's house, and to Jasper's. He noticed a few people peeking out their windows, but no one tried to stop them. As soon as he was parked, he and Turner were out of the car, rushing inside Jasper's house.

Raven barked out a laugh when they found him. He wasn't unconscious or dead like Raven had been afraid, but rather, pissed.

"Untie me," he said through gritted teeth.

Someone, possibly Jasper's father, had tied him up to a chair.

"We were worried about you," Raven said as he went to work.

"I'm going to fucking kill him," Jasper said with a growl.

"That's not going to be hard, considering the state he's in."

"What happened?"

"He tried to attack the badgers, but Turner kicked his ass. That was why we were delayed. I apologize, Alpha Rhodes."

Jasper shuddered. "Don't call me that."

"But you're the alpha now. Your father isn't coming back. I don't think he'll ever leave the council's jail once this is over. That makes you the alpha."

"I have no idea what to do."

Raven clasped his shoulder. "You don't have to know right now. You'll be fine, though."

Raven truly believed that. He might not know Jasper well, but he knew him enough to be sure that Jasper would be a better alpha than his father.

Of course, that wouldn't be too hard. Anyone with common decency would be a better alpha than Jasper's father.

EPILOGUE

"What do you think?" Turner asked.

Raven came to stand behind him. He wrapped his arms around Turner's waist and pulled him close, and Turner went willingly. They stared at the painting on the wall for a moment, Turner holding his breath and hoping Raven would like it.

"It's nice," Raven eventually said.

Turner snorted. "Do you want me to take it down?"

"No. I don't hate it, even though it's not really my thing. It's yours, and I want you to feel at home here."

"I do." Turner turned around in Raven's arms and hugged him. "This is my home now."

The smile Raven gave him was worth taking the painting off the wall.

Three weeks had passed since Rhodes had tried to attack the badgers. Since then, Turner had moved in with Raven. He'd endured teasing from his friends, but he wouldn't have had it any other way.

Joel had been pissed when he'd seen him after Turner had snuck out of the house. He'd yelled at him for ten minutes before hugging him and telling him never to scare him again. Turner had promised, and they were back to being fast friends. All the other carriers had been more amused than angry, although they'd been terrified, at least the ones who'd been in Thomas's house when Rhodes's men had attacked. It had reminded them of other situations in which they'd been vulnerable, and a few were still trying to deal with that.

The carriers who'd stayed back at the Bishop house were all okay, though. Misha had given birth, and Turner had never seen him happier. Misha kept insisting it was because he was finally not pregnant anymore and could hug his baby, but Turner suspected it also had a lot to do with the human who kept visiting the Bishop house. He'd have to ask Misha about it the next time they saw each other.

As for Rhodes, he was behind bars. After Thomas had told the council what Rhodes had done, they'd locked his ass up faster than Rhodes had been able to protest, and while they hadn't yet officially decided what his punishment would be, everyone knew he wasn't going anywhere. The cell he was in would be his home for years to come, which was perfectly fine with Turner. Rhodes should never see the light of day again, and if the council changed their mind about him, Turner would be right there, telling them how stupid it was.

"Anyone home?" a voice called out from the entrance.

Raven scrunched his nose. "Why is he always here? Doesn't he have a surfeit to lead?"

Turner kissed him before stepping out of his embrace. "He's our friend."

"Still. I feel like I haven't had you to myself in too long."

Turner felt the same way, but they'd have time. They had the rest of their lives to be together, and besides, he wanted to help Jasper.

Jasper had become the skunk alpha after his father had been imprisoned. The problem was that he had no idea what he was doing. His father had never taught him how to lead, which might have not been a bad thing considering how bad an alpha he'd been. It meant Jasper had to figure things out on his own, though, which wasn't easy. That was why he visited cete territory so often. He spent a lot of time with Thomas, who gave him tips and tried to help him untangle what his father had done to the surfeit. It would take time, but Turner had faith in Jasper.

"In the living room," he called out.

Jasper appeared only seconds later. He looked tired, which wasn't surprising. It worried Turner a bit, and he pointed at the couch.

"Sit down."

Jasper flopped onto the couch with a relieved sigh. "I'm so freaking tired," he complained.

"Stay for dinner," Turner said. He didn't ask if Raven was okay with it. He already knew Raven would be.

Jasper rubbed his face. "I can't believe how many things I have to deal with now that I'm the alpha. I wasn't ready for any of this. Thomas introduced me to the humans who live in the forest today, and I had no idea what to do or say."

"They're just normal people, like us."

"I know that. I was terrified they'd told their bosses what my father did."

Turner sat next to him. "They didn't?"

"No. The guy in charge, Luther, said it was none of their business. I'm not sure why."

"That's because he's dating Josiah."

"Right. He's the other father of Josiah's baby?"

"Exactly. That means he wants the other humans to leave us alone as much as possible. It's one of the reasons everyone was so happy when he and his team became our liaison with the humans. He cares about Josiah and the forest, which means he'll keep our secrets."

Raven had disappeared into the kitchen, no doubt making coffee. Turner suspected he was giving him and Jasper time to talk. Turner was never sure how to behave around Jasper, but now that he wasn't part of the surfeit anymore, it was easier.

"Thomas told me there are talks about opening the forest," Jasper said. "Can you believe that? I don't think I'd want to leave this place even if I could."

"You, maybe not, but others might decide to do just that. I think it's good they'll have the opportunity, although I know it won't happen anytime soon." Turner had no intention of ever leaving, just like Jasper. His world might be restricted to the forest, but it was more than big enough for him. He felt safe here, finally, and ready to start his life.

Turner had everything and everyone he needed here in the forest. He'd almost lost it because he hadn't realized it, but he'd never make that mistake again.

ABOUT THE AUTHOR

Catherine is the creator of several series, most of them paranormal, including the Whitedell Pride Series and the Gillham Pack Series. While she graduated in translation, she decided to go the writer's way because it was more fun to create her own stories and characters.

She's been living in Italy for more than twenty years, but she's a daughter of the North—Belgium to be precise—and she misses it so much that she's already planning to move back.

She loves pizza—probably too much—her son, her pets, and of course, books. She sneaks some reading time into her schedule every time she has five minutes free from writing, demands from her various pets and son, and lastly, housework.

Connect with her:

lievens.catherine@gmail.com
BookBub: https://www.bookbub.com/authors/catherine-lievens
Website: https://authorcatherinelievens.com/
Facebook: https://www.facebook.com/catherine.lievens.9
Facebook Group: https://www.facebook.com/groups/411778002341528/
Twitter: https://twitter.com/authorCLievens
Newsletter: http://eepurl.com/c-uvKn